HIGH JINX

The Perpetrators

Mohonk Mysteries

High Jinx
Transylvania Station
The Hood House Heist
Double Crossing
Way Out, West
The Maltese Herring

HIGH JINX

Donald & Abby
Westlake

Cover by Edward Gorey and Joe Servello;
back cover by Joe Servello

FIRST EDITION
Published December 1987

Dennis McMillan Publications
1995 Calais Dr. No. 3
Miami Beach, FL 33141

Distributed by Creative Arts Book Co.
833 Bancroft Way
Berkeley, CA 94710

Acknowledgements

We wish to thank the many people whose wit and work made it possible for us to stand up here as though we'd done the whole thing ourselves.

First, to Dilys Winn and Carol Brener, who thought it up and ironed the bugs out and turned it over to us as a wonderful surprise package.

And to our speakers and suspects, all of whom have taken this friviolity just seriously enough to make it work.

And then, at Mohonk Mountain House, pre-eminently to Faire Hart, who runs the program for the hotel and saves our lives at least once a day, without ever losing her optimism.

And to Barbara Seaman and Carol Schimmer, also of Mohonk, who ignore both the clock and good sense and just get the job done.

And to Annie O'Neill, graphics designer *par excellence,* who gives each Weekend its distinctive look.

And to Matthew Seaman, a skilled and imaginative cameraman/photographer/director, who every year takes our rough notes for Thursday night's narration and turns them into smooth and evocative visuals, whether film or slides.

And to the cheerful and high-spirited employees of Mohonk, who in their time have been, at our request, everything from cowboys to Transylvanian villagers.

Thank you!

The Business

The Mohonk Mysteries are the property of Donald E. and Abby Westlake and Mohonk Mountain House. They may not be presented or performed for profit.

For permission for a non-profit organization to present or perform a Mohonk Mystery, write to the publisher on your organization's letterhead.

The photos on pages 20, 22, 28, 30, 32 & 70 are by Abby Westlake. The photo on page 62 is by Knox Burger. All other photos are by Matthew Seaman, and are the property of Matthew Seaman and Mohonk Mountain House.

Foreword

In January of 1977, two ingenious women named Dilys Winn and Carol Brener put on, at a huge and magnificently rustic mountaintop hotel ninety miles north of New York City, the world's first mystery weekend, in which the guests were invited to observe and then solve a murder. Celebrity speakers that first year included Isaac Asimov and Phyllis Whitney, and the idea was so successful it became an annual affair, and has bred imitators by now from California to the British Isles.

We'd heard of the Mohonk Mystery Weekends, but had never seen one in action until Dilys, by then running the program herself, invited us to observe the sixth in the series, *The Teacup Caper,* featuring Ruth Rendell and Frederick "Dial M for Murder" Knott. When it was over, she told us she was running out of steam and felt she needed someone else to take over. Would we? We would.

The Weekend by then had been moved to March, and was the most popular annual event at Mohonk Mountain House. The first Thursday of each December, the hotel switchboard would be opened at nine A.M. to accept Mystery reservations for the following March. Before noon on that day, the Weekend would be filled (that's more than three hundred people), with a one hundred name waiting list. The competition is so intense that there have been as many as fifty people staying at Mohonk on the Wednesday night before that reservation Thursday, simply to be at the desk the next morning to be sure of a place.

Reacting to that pressure, our third year in charge we doubled to two consecutive Mystery Weekends, with the same suspects and speakers but with the story slightly changed the second time around. And there's *still* a waiting list every December, on reservation day.

We've made some other changes, too. We still sort the guests (shall we call them *quests?* Yes) into competing teams, but we've started giving two first-place prizes. We feel there are two separate impulses at work among the quests; there are those who want to *solve the puzzle,* want to walk in the footsteps of Sherlock Holmes and Nero Wolfe; and there are those who want to take the story elements we offer and *run amok,* playing off the conventions just as much as we do. To give opportunity to both motives, we offer one team a prize for the most accurate solution and one for the most creative. And it is amazing just how much manic creativity you can unleash from three hundred bright happy people isolated for a weekend on a mountaintop.

Another change we've made is in the prizes themselves. The glory of winning has always been and still is the main award, and we still give token physical prizes as well, but we've added a prize the people really seem to like: The members of the two winning teams get to jump next year's line. If they want to come back—and most do—they have a guaranteed reservation. At our most recent Weekend, a man on a losing team was heard to say, when the winners were announced, "Damn! Back to dialing."

* * *

What is this Mystery Weekend, that people love it so? Let us describe it, step by step; not the same as being there, but just to give the idea.

The Weekend begins on Thursday, which in terms of weekends is already a plus. The quests arrive in mid-afternoon, and after dinner they meet the mystery, in the form either of a slide show or a film, with accompanying narration. Here they see the murder victim's last day, the people he/she meets, the locations, the period, the *style*.

The murder victim's last day will include encounters with ten to twelve other people, the suspects in the story. For two hours on Friday, one in the morning and one in the afternoon, these suspects are available for interrogation. The rule of the game is that the suspects *must always* tell the truth, except that the murderer will lie about the murder. (Not about motive; even the murderer will tell the truth about that. The physical facts of the murder is the only area of lies.) On the other hand, the suspects will not volunteer information; the quests have to figure out which are the right questions to ask.

On Friday night, or some time on Saturday, there's usually some other event that moves the story along. Sometime's it's a second murder, sometimes something else. (In *Transylvania Station,* Madame Openskya graciously consented to conduct a seance, during which the murder victim appeared, making that the only Weekend so far in which the quests could interrogate the victim.) And finally, on Sunday morning, the teams are asked to present their solutions, and the more elaborate the presentation, the better.

That's the bare bones of the program, but there are other diversions along the way. We always have four or five speakers to talk on subjects connected with the theme of that Weekend. These have ranged from Will Shortz, senior editor of *Games* magazine, who spoke on puzzle-solving, through cartoonist Gahan Wilson and British newspaper columnist Katharine Whitehorn, to John and Mary Maxtone-Graham, he the author of the definitive history of the trans-Atlantic passenger liners, *The Only Way to Cross,* who spoke during our ocean-voyage mystery, *Double Crossing.*

Of course, mystery and thriller writers have been prominent among our suspect/speakers. In our first five years, these included Robert Byrne, Max Allan Collins, Brian Garfield, Joe Gores, Stephen King, Peter Lovesey, Gavin Lyall, David Morrell, Edward A. Pollitz, Jr., Justin Scott, Martin Cruz Smith and Peter Straub. And on the real-life side of crime and detection, Marie Castoire told us how it felt to be a female homicide detective in Manhattan, and her husband, Mike Gatto, also a New York cop, told us some of *his* experiences.

From the beginning, Edward Gorey has set the mood by doing the theme drawing for every Weekend's brochure. And film scholar Chris Steinbrunner chooses appropriate movies to be run every night of the Weekend, with commentary by himself.

Although a few professional actors have been suspects, our usual approach is to use amateurs. (The actors were there as friends, not as pros.) Abby has been a suspect, though Don has not. Our guest speakers are always dragooned into being suspects, and we've used our friends and family as well, plus a number of employees of the hotel. We *want* the teams to feel they can put on as good a show as we can; a lot of the time, they put on a better one.

* * *

The preparation of a Mystery Weekend is unlike any other kind of storytelling we can think of, but it's storytelling. What makes it different is that it's a story told in fits and starts, by misdirection and repetition, and with such a lushness of narrative— and profusion of red herrings (and red hearings)— that the same story can be twisted into two separate solutions on the two consecutive weekends. And the way we put this story together is probably as unusual as the form itself.

First we determine the germ of an idea, a sense of what our story will be. Armed with that, we shoot our film or slides and write the accompanying narration. Then we write our suspect biographies, telling each suspect, "This is who you are and this is what you know." The suspects are not told the whole story, only their part in it, which means the suspects get some surprises, too, during the interrogations. And finally we write the full story of the mystery, the Truth.

This piecemeal creation is echoed in the piecemeal unleashing of the story during the Mystery Weekend, beginning with the narrated film or slides, the interrogations, whatever other event we've thrown in to keep the story moving, and culminating on Sunday morning, when the teams of quests tell their versions of the story back to us in their own way, with singing and dancing and bad puns and little playlets and costumes and signs and props and general hilarity. After which, to close the Weekend, we tell them the Truth.

This book is a recreation of such a Mohonk Mystery Weekend, or as close as we can come to the real thing on the printed page. The book is divided into four sections, approximating the experience of the Weekend:

1. The Narration. This is the narration Don gives on Thursday evening, accompanying the film or slides.

2. The Suspect Biographies. This, in a slightly modified form, is what each suspect is given before the Weekend. Some repetition here is inevitable, because at least two people will know virtually every fact or event in the story.

3. The Quiz. We don't have this quiz at the Weekend itself, because the quests are interacting with the suspects and the events, and are presenting their solutions in their own way. We tried to think of an equivalent to those presentations, and this is it. Abby has done a number of magazine quizzes, so she's adapted that form and our story-form and fitted them together.

4. The Truth. This, again in a slightly modified form, is what we tell the quests at the end of the Weekend.

The Mohonk Mystery Weekends did not begin as stories to be read, but as stories to be told and retold and searched for and adapted from and played with like Silly Putty. The idea of it is *story* as *game*. We hope we've made the transition successfully to a more or less normal narrative, but it needn't end there. It's still a game, and you're invited to play.

Happy solving!

Introduction
by
Martin Cruz Smith

At an unlikely time of the year—mid-March, "mud season" in New York State—and at an unlikely site—the grand Victorian resort of Mohonk, a spa of Quaker sobriety—writers and readers of whodunits gather for Donald Westlake's 'Mystery Weekends.' Readers reserve their rooms a year in advance. Writers fly in from faraway countries like Great Britain and California.

Why? Let's suppose that, finally, readers have their opportunity to be Marlowe, Spade, Miss Marple. To be gumshoe, cop, inspired detective; to dish it out instead of merely reading about it. Writers, it must be assumed, are satisfying a perverse need to be suspects, to roar like Greenstreet, to whine like Lorre. Or worse (or better, depending on your point of view) to be the killer, to finally rise from the typewriter, pick up the letter opener and . . . But I'm getting ahead of myself.

Which isn't hard. For months I had begged Donald to give me some idea of the character I would play in the upcoming *High Jinx* so I could gather information and wallow in character. Those of us who are not professional actors need all the wallowing we can muster. Mustering anxiety is no problem at all. Every mirror was a casting agent.

High Jinx. Could be anything. Could be a snow-bound train in the Rockies. Time, 1880's. I could be an Indian scout, Cheyenne, Shoshone. Or a cruise ship in the Mediterranean. Time, 1950's. I could be Italian, a lover at night, a killer during the day.

At last, a letter dropped like a limp body through my mail slot. It said, "You are Leopold Schmendrick, a ship's architect from Kiel." In three pages, Westlake limned my new Schmendreckian persona, evoked the Nazi era our drama was taking place in, damned the character of the villian ('Kurt Krauss, the most hated critic in Germany'), reviewed the other dozen suspects and delivered a plot no less complicated than a schematic of the Hindenberg.

I had, by my digital watch, about 12 hours to buy the Michelin for Germany (where is Kiel?), steal a book on yacht construction (know the difference between batten and a duck) and learn Hoch Deutsch (or, at least, concoct an accent more German than, say, Spanish). The main point, however, was that I was going to play someone called Leopold Schmendrick, and Schmendrick was a shnook.

This was an agony not anticipated, to be a character in the hands of another writer. Worse, a minor character. Yes, we're all willing to kill or be killed. Hell is to be an also-ran. For the first time I sympathized with so many of the characters I'd created, the 'usual suspects' brought to life just to mislead readers. Not that I hated Donald. I just wondered if my characters felt towards me the way I felt towards Donald. Schmendrick, indeed.

Not that the teams of 'detectives' who swarmed over the 'suspects' seemed to care. They had come to Mohonk because their fantasies were far better than ours. In real life in Texas or Manhattan they might have been teachers or housewives, brokers or Bible salesmen. As *High Jinx* interrogators they fell into two categories. The trial lawyers (a composite Perry Mason-Poirot). And a small but substantial group, both male and female, who betrayed the bad cop's impulse to reach for a rubber hose.

Actually, some of us were pretty good. Ed Pollitz made a proto-Fascist police captain, complete in monocle and patent leather helmet, who set the audience's blood to boil. There were interrogators who were actually spitting at him. Gavin Lyall was impenetrably British. His wife, Katharine Whitehorn, played a journalist of a ladylike charm and sly cunning that explained her own distinguished career on the London *Observer*. Abby Westlake played a nanny described in the letter I received as "sweet and ditzy." Abby is Don's wife. I don't know what he told her she was playing.

As for Leopold Schmendrick all I can say is that he tried. Since the mystery was played on two successive weekends, Leopold had hopes of being promoted to homicidal maniac. The only real development was that by the end of the second weekend my German accent sounded like a man speaking through a mouth full of tapioca pudding.

No matter. I can't recall ever seeing so many people so continuously giddy, from interrogation to costume ball to Sunday's presentation of solutions. Some solutions were impressively logical, some were musical, some were unprintable. The terrifying thing was, if Donald would have let us, I think we were all willing to do it all over again.

And I know Leopold has it in him to kill someone sometime.

The Speakers

Gavin Lyall, suspense novelist, author of *The Most Dangerous Game* and the Major Maxim series.

Edward A. Pollitz, Jr., financier/businessman and suspense novelist under both his own name and Nick Christian.

Martin Cruz Smith, author of *Gorky Park, Nightwing* and *Stallion Gate.*

Katharine Whitehorn, reporter and columnist with the London *Observer.*

The Cast

Professor Rudolf Diederich, Wingate Hart
Ingrid Diedrich, Jana Notick
Frau Freya Frage, Faire Hart
Joslyn Frank, Katharine Whitehorn
Marty Hollands, Greg Garrick
Kurt Krauss, Jim Thompson
Basil Naunton, Knox Burger
Gelda Pourboire, Daniele Pollitz
Miss Olivia Quaile, Abby Westlake
Wayne Radford, Gavin Lyall
Leopold Schmendrick, Martin Cruz Smith
Hama Tartus, Frank Hamilton
Captain Wilhelm Trehn, Edward A. Pollitz, Jr.

The Scene: The snowbound Hotel Kuckkuckuhr, high atop Mont Melblanc in the Swiss Alps.

The Time: 1938

Hama Tartus and Frau Freya Frage

The Narration

Europe, 1938!

All across the continent the terrible tension built, rising inexorably toward the winds of war. Fear and hatred slashed this way, and then fear and hatred slashed that way, with only a few little Bandaids of effort to repair the damage.

In one small spot called Switzerland, in the very center of Europe, there was still peace.

And snow.

All around the mountaintop hotel called Kuckkuc-kuhr the snow piles high. Storms and avalanches have cut off the thirteen people within, isolating them. No one can leave, and no other person can join the group.

Certainly no employee of the hotel can make it up the mountain from Käseberg, the little town far below. So that means there are only two people in the hotel to care for the eleven guests. Hama Tartus, the owner, has to cook and serve dinner himself. He is assisted only by his assistant, Frau Freya Frage.

Marty Hollands

The young American mystery writer, Marty Hollands, is the first to come down to dine this evening. His manner is chipper and friendly. He seems open and eager for experience, with a smile for everyone.

Another early arrival is the retired nanny, Miss Olivia Quaile. A pleasant old body, Miss Quaile likes to chat about most anything with everybody she meets.

She is followed in the dining room by Herr Professor Rudolf Diederich, who is here with his grown daughter, Ingrid. Both father and daughter seem quite sad and distracted. Their clothing is shabby, their manner pessimistic.

Two ladies traveling alone next enter the dining room, and choose to dine together. One is the British journalist Joslyn Frank, a self-contained and practical woman, and the other is French singer/actress Gelda Pourboire, who sweeps into the room with flair and self-assurance, but whose aura of glamour seems just a trifle tattered around the edges.

As these people enjoy their appetizers, brought to them by the hardworking Hama Tartus and Frau Freya Frage, all seems peaceful at the Kuckkuckuhr Hotel. And then there arrives . . .

Kurt Krauss

Kurt Krauss.

The most feared . . . critic in all Europe.

With the flick of an eyebrow, Kurt Krauss can close a play, damn a book, destroy a career. A man of gargantuan appetites, Kurt Krauss speaks with authority in the worlds of the novel, the theater, the movies, the dance. He is also, on occasion, a producer of films and plays. His having been an early and enthusiastic member of the Nazi Party also helps. Gourmet, gourmand and glutton, Kurt Krauss is a powerful man indeed.

Hama Tartus seats Krauss at the table in the corner, nearest the entrance. With his back to the corner, Krauss can see and be seen by everybody else in the room.

The first course is brought to the coldly appreciative Kurt Krauss by Frau Freya Frage.

As Krauss settles down to eat, local police captain Wilhelm Trehn appears. The stout and sinister Captain Trehn seems very interested in the presence of the much stouter and more sinister Kurt Krauss and would like some sort of conversation with the man. He even sits briefly at the table with Krauss, attempting to talk with him.

But Krauss is not at all interested in dinnertime chat with Captain Trehn, which he makes very obvious, brushing Trehn off like a bothersome fly. Clearly miffed, Captain Trehn goes to his own table, which he is to share with young American mystery writer Marty Hollands. Hollands and the Captain politely introduce themselves to one another.

Wayne Radford and Basil Naunton

The next arrivals are a pair of enthusiastic sports fans, Wayne Radford and Basil Naunton. They seem surprised but moderately pleased to see Kurt Krauss, and crowd briefly around his table, with cheerful words and manly offers to shake hands.

But they too are rejected by Krauss, who glares at them over his food and makes shooing gestures to get them away from his table. Frau Freya Frage hustles the sportsmen off to their own table, where they ask her to plug in their radio. While eating, they like to listen to the sports scores from all over the world.

As the sportsmen lean over their radio, trying to hear through the static caused by the storm outside, the last of the players in our drama arrives. One Leopold Schmendrick, he is a nervous and harried man indeed. When he sees Kurt Krauss he seems very agitated, as though he's in deep trouble and hopes Krauss will help him. In his urgency, he stumbles against Krauss's table, and nearly spills Krauss's beer.

Schmendrick, too, is waved away by the irascible Krauss. As Captain Trehn watches with great interest, Hama Tartus leads the nervous Schmendrick away and seats him with the sweet little old lady, Miss Olivia Quaile, who immediately starts to chat with him. Despite her kindly efforts, however, Schmendrick continues to look deeply gloomy and distressed.

Captain Wilhelm Trehn

Our cast is completely assembled now, thirteen people in one dining room in a hotel completely surrounded by snow, cut off by storms and avalanches. Outside, the storm continues, the snow piling ever deeper, closing the passes, blocking the roads. The worst winter storm in Swiss history has arrived.

As the diners, principally Kurt Krauss, continue to dine in the warm comfort of the hotel, police captain Wilhelm Trehn follows Hama Tartus into the kitchen for a private conversation. What would the Captain have in mind?

Another person on the move is Miss Olivia Quaile. With a gentle, "Excuse me," to her tablemate, Leopold Schmendrick, she rises and crosses the room, carrying with her a map which she wants to show Kurt Krauss. He doesn't want to see the map, he wants to see his food, but she keeps holding it close to him, showing him . . . Schleswig-Holstein.

No. He's eating a Holstein, leave him alone. No matter how Miss Quaile tries, Krauss just won't have anything to do with her and her map, so at last she turns away, crushed by rejection, and slowly returns to her table in tears, poor lady, where she is consoled in the best manner he can summon by Leopold Schmendrick.

In the meantime, Captain Wilhelm Trehn, looking quite satisfied with himself, returns from the kitchen, while owner Hama Tartus has a perhaps unhappy word to say in the ear of Leopold Schmendrick, who reacts by looking even gloomier than before.

**Professor Rudolf Diederich and
Ingrid Diederich**

As all of these undercurrents and tensions heat up within, relationships barely hinted at, the snow stays cold and deep without. Perhaps, before dinner ends, something will happen to break the tension within?

If so, Kurt Krauss seems unaware of any impending trouble. He continues to eat, course after course, until Joslyn Frank, the British journalist, comes over from the table she's been sharing with Gelda Pourboire. Joslyn Frank's pencil and notepad are at the ready as she calmly seats herself at Krauss's table, makes space for herself among his plates and glasses, and lets it be known she has a question or two to ask the powerful Mr. Krauss.

Joslyn Frank is quite forceful in her style of asking questions, but Kurt Krauss is equally forceful about not answering them. A glare is all the determined reporter gets in return for her efforts.

Young American mystery writer Marty Hollands notices this contretemps, which soon ends with Joslyn Frank, obviously irritated, returning to her own table, her questions unanswered. Her tablemate, the French singer/actress Gelda Pourboire, seems very displeased with Kurt Krauss and glares in his direction, but Krauss pays no attention to anything but more and more food.

Young Marty Hollands' attention soon shifts from the scene of bad temper. Gazing across the room with a tender smile, he catches the eye of young Ingrid Diederich, daughter of Professor Diederich. For just that moment, her sadness seems to lift, and she shyly lowers her head with a faint smile.

Captain Trehn, seated with Marty Hollands, notices this exchange between the young couple and seems benevolently amused by it.

Gelda Pourboire

But Gelda Pourboire has now decided not to let this slight to her dinner companion pass unremarked. Getting to her feet, she marches across to Kurt Krauss, interrupting his meal yet again. With withering scorn, she loudly informs him what she thinks of him, continuing until Frau Freya Frage hurries from the kitchen, startled and nervous, to make Gelda return to her own table.

Krauss, with a heavy glare around the room, shakes his head at this latest interruption, and returns to his meal.

Herr Professor Diederich and his daughter, having finished their small meal, stand and prepare to leave the dining room. Marty Hollands rises to bow them out, smiling at both father and daughter, but perhaps just a bit more at the daughter. The Diederichs smile and bow back, then move on toward the door, both slow and careworn.

Just as they are passing Kurt Krauss's table, Ingrid falters! She seems about to faint. Staggering to the side, she collapses half on Krauss's table and half on the empty chair facing him. The Professor does his best to help her, but he too is obviously very weak, and he shows his gratitude when Marty Hollands rushes over to help the poor girl onto her feet once more.

As for Krauss, the milk of human kindness is not in him. He doesn't care how weak and pitiful Ingrid Diederich might be; all he wants is for these people to go away and let him eat. He waves boorishly at them, grunting his displeasure.

Marty doesn't like that attitude at all, and he leans across Krauss's table to tell him so, firmly and at length, before seeing the Diederichs to the door and returning to his own table to finish his meal.

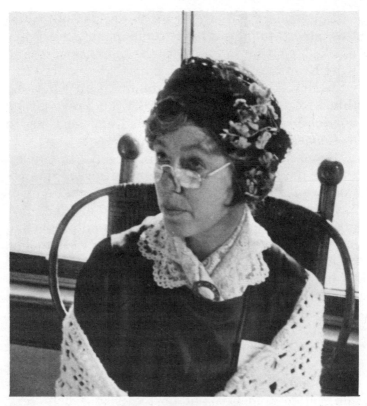

Miss Olivia Quaile

Gelda Pourboire and Joslyn Frank now both leave the room, Joslyn ignoring Krauss and Gelda giving him a haughty look, which Krauss seems not to notice.

Sportsmen Wayne Radford and Basil Naunton, having finished their meal, gather up their radio and prepare to leave. Miss Olivia Quaile joins them, showing them the map Krauss wouldn't look at, and the three depart together.

Hama Tartus has been waiting in the kitchen doorway for Marty Hollands to leave, and when the young man finally does, Tartus hurries to Hollands' tablemate, Captain Wilhelm Trehn. From his manner as he stoops over the captain, Tartus is begging Trehn to reconsider whatever villainy he's planning. From Trehn's smug and self-satisfied look, he is not about to reconsider anything. Finally Tartus throws his hands up, admitting defeat, and returns to the kitchen.

Trehn looks across the room at Leopold Schmendrick, who seems to wilt under that gaze. Crooking one finger, Trehn beckons Schmendrick to come join him, and with great reluctance Schmendrick obeys, crossing to take the seat vacated by Marty Hollands.

These two very different people, Captain Wilhelm Trehn and Leopold Schmendrick, speak briefly and then both rise. Trehn rests a heavy hand on Schmendrick's shoulder as he leads him from the room, making it clear that Schmendrick now belongs to the law. The sad Hama Tartus and Frau Freya Frage stand in the kitchen doorway and watch.

Ten people have dined here tonight, and finished, and gone away. One still eats, and guess who! Kurt Krauss has now finally and at last reached dessert, however, a huge bowl of tapioca pudding. Hama Tartus and Frau Freya Frage exit to the kitchen, leaving Krauss alone in the dining room, when . . . all at once . . .

Kurt Krauss topples forward into his tapioca!

Kurt Krauss is dead!

* * *

Who poisoned Kurt Krauss?

Was it Frau Freya Frage, serving his soup?

Was it Captain Wilhelm Trehn, attempting to converse with Krauss and not used to being brushed aside?

Was it the sportsmen, Wayne Radford and Basil Naunton, during their bluff and hearty greeting of the critic?

Was it Leopold Schmendrick, while begging for help?

Was it Hama Tartus, who prepared all the food?

Was it Miss Olivia Quaile, while showing her map of Schleswig-Holstein?

Was it Joslyn Frank, while clearing a space on Krauss's table for her pencil and notebook?

Was it her fiery dinner companion, Gelda Pourboire, while giving Krauss a piece of her mind?

Was it Professor Diederich, or his daughter Ingrid, while she was fainting?

Was it young mystery writer Marty Hollands, while objecting to Krauss's boorishness toward the Diederichs?

Whoever it was, somebody poisoned Kurt Krauss, and it is absolutely certain that that somebody is
       still
           in
               this
                    hotel.

High Jinx Biographies—Proem

Every Mystery Weekend is unique in one way or another. *High Jinx* is the only one in which a number of the suspects immediately confessed the murder! Which startled the quests, as you may imagine.

In order to adapt to this unusual circumstance, we bent the basic rule slightly. The basic rule is that everyone must tell the truth, except that the murderer will lie about the murder. For *High Jinx,* and only for *High Jinx,* we altered the rule:

Every suspect must tell the truth about everything, except that *anybody* may lie about the murder. The murderer may claim innocence, or guilt. Everyone else has the same option.

This added an interesting complexity to the case. Not only did the quests have to figure out which—if any—of the confessions was truthful, they also had to figure out what motivated the innocent suspects to confess to a murder they had not committed.

And now you have that same conundrum. Enjoy!

Biographies

Marty Hollands

I killed Kurt Krauss and I don't care who knows it.

I'm a detective story writer, originally from Cleveland, Ohio. Some of the books I've written are: *Blood on the Doorknob, Murder on the Trolley, Evil on the Menu.* Four years ago film rights to those three books were optioned by a German producer—named Kurt Krauss. The movies were made and released in Germany, but I was never paid the money due me. I tried, unsuccessfully, to track down Mr. Krauss from the U.S., but he pulled a vanishing act. I finally decided to come to Europe, and to combine my search for Kurt Krauss with another project, research into the Schleswig-Holstein Question for a book I'm writing, a historical to be titled *Stain on the Pedigree.*

I've had so many adventures since I came to Europe, I feel like I'm living in one of my novels! The first was about two months ago. I was on a train traveling from France to Kiel, in Germany, when I met a very glamorous young lady from France named Gelda Pourboire. She was on her way to Kiel also, because she had a job there singing in a nightclub. We shared a bottle of wine and then we shared my bunk, and all in all it was a pretty swell way to pass the time. I didn't see her again until last night when she turned up in the Hotel Kuckkuckuhr. I was a little surprised to see her here because she'd told me she expected to be working in Kiel for a long time.

In Kiel, I learned there was a naval scientist at the university there, Professor Rudolf Diederich, whose hobby was the Schleswig-Holstein Question. Naturally I wanted to visit with him, but when I went to his house there were soldiers guarding it. The prof was under house arrest because he'd rubbed the Nazis the wrong way, and he wasn't allowed out and I wasn't allowed in.

Well, no one's going to tell Marty Hollands who he can or can't visit. The next day I bribed the mailman to let me borrow his uniform and I had my first visit with the prof. That's when I met his daughter Ingrid, a really swell girl, probably the prettiest young lady in Germany. Ingrid and her dad (Mrs. Diederich passed on when Ingrid was a baby) have been cooped up in that house for five years.

I went back to see them several times, disguised as the water-meter reader, the butcher's delivery boy, the plumber, and so on. The prof and I talked about Schleswig-Holstein, and I fell in love with Ingrid. She was too depressed by their long confinement to notice me, so I didn't press the matter.

One day they told me that the person responsible for their captivity was none other than Kurt Krauss. He had denounced the prof because one of his Nazi pals wanted Diederich's position at the university. The swine! When I realized that the Diederichs had also been injured by this Krauss guy, I decided it was my mission to rescue them.

The next day I showed up disguised as the dog-catcher, complete with his caged truck. I told the guards a rabid dog had been seen hiding under the porch. They stayed well away as I backed the truck up to the house. I distracted the guards while the

Diederichs, wearing fur coats, slipped into the back of the truck. Then I drove them away and we made our way across Germany toward Switzerland.

Only once was I really worried: We were stuck behind a slow-moving circus, southbound, its trucks and wagons filling the small secondary road we were on. And, at the same time, a large Army staff car was directly behind us, full of uniformed officers! At last the road widened, and the staff car rushed by us with a great blasting of its horn, the military men paying no attention to us at all. Once they were gone, I drove more carefully past the circus—a seedy run-down affair, with the name "Rundelman's" on the flapping canvas sides of the wagons—and without further incident we raced on to Switzerland.

Where we came straight to this hotel. Frau Freya Frage, the housekeeper here, used to work for the prof, and they knew they'd be safe with her. That was three days ago. I've contacted friends back home and hope to be able to get them to the United States, where they can live in peace and freedom and prosperity, and where hopefully, one day Ingrid will return my love.

There are several people here in Kuckkuckuhr whom I've seen before. Those two sporty types, Wayne Radford and Basil Naunton, were staying at the Hotel Splendide in Kiel, at the same time I was there. And that little old lady, Olivia Quaile, was also at the Splendide. She's one of those indefatigable tourists who has to personally visit every inch of whatever foreign place she's in. She had maps of the coastline and she used to pester me to tell her about the various sights. Radford and Naunton are friendly chaps—I used to see them in the bar at the Splendide.

Last night we four renewed our acquaintance when we met in the sitting room before dinner. Wayne Radford and Basil Naunton regaled us with anecdotes about their travels. On the way here they'd witnessed an odd incident; the same traveling circus we had seen was stopped by the police in Germany, just before the Swiss border, and the Gestapo hauled away the midget. The two sportsmen found this highly amusing, but after my own experiences with the Diederichs I didn't see much humor in the story, and I sensed Miss Quaile was quite offended, although she was too much of a lady to say so.

There were two women in the dining room last night whom I also recognized. I saw Joslyn Frank in Kiel a couple of times—she and Olivia Quaile used to go sightseeing together, in Miss Frank's car. Joslyn Frank and I had corresponded a while back, because she wrote a book, *Who Cares Who Killed Schleswig-Holstein?* that I consulted in the course of my research, but we've never been introduced. And sitting at the table with her was none other than Gelda Pourboire—whom I had spent that memorable night with on the train. I was awful embarrassed to see her here, in the same room with the prof and Ingrid, but she didn't say anything to me, so I reckon my secret is safe. The others—Hama Tartus, Mrs. Freya Frage, Leopold Schmendrick, and the policeman, Captain Trehn—are all new to me.

I sat with Captain Trehn. I thought it best to let Ingrid and the prof sit by themselves. They're very shy and nervous, as who wouldn't be after all they've been through. I was a little uneasy about the cop, that he'd make trouble for the Diederichs.

It was Captain Trehn who told me that the fat

guy was none other than Kurt Krauss! I happened to have some poison in my pocket (I was conducting an experiment as research for one of my books) and on impulse I decided to drop it into Krauss's goulash. I thought it would be a real good thing to rid the world of this despicable human being. When the Diederichs got up to leave the dining room I followed. Luckily I was there to catch poor Ingrid when she fainted, overcome by fear and loathing at the sight of Mr. Krauss. Her faint gave me the opportunity I needed to sprinkle the poison on Krauss's plate.

We then retired to our separate rooms and I was just preparing for bed when Captain Trehn came to announce Krauss's death. Good riddance to bad rubbish, I say!

**Professor Rudolf Diederich responds
thoughtfully to interrogation.**

Herr Professor
Rudolf Diederich

It was I, Rudolf Diederich, who killed Kurt Krauss.

I am a naval scientist, a member of the faculty of the University of Kiel. Until 1933 I was doing work on some very advanced submarines. I had invented the R-boat, the S-boat and the T-boat when my research was interrupted. I was denounced to the Nazis and, together with my 15-year old daughter, Ingrid— my wife, Ingrid's mother, died many years ago— placed under house arrest. There we remained, isolated from the outer world, until a few days ago.

Early in our captivity, in a letter from a colleague which was smuggled into the house in a package of bratwurst, I learned the identity of my denouncer: It was Kurt Krauss, the infamous critic; his motive, the wish to install one of his Nazi cronies in my chair at the university.

For the first three years, our lonely exile was shared by a kind-hearted woman, Frau Freya Frage, who served as our housekeeper. She was close to the family, almost a mother to my poor daughter, Ingrid. Then tragedy struck. Frau Freya's husband, Felix Frage, who was a sea cook, died in a drowning accident. Not long afterward she left Kiel to start a new life here in Switzerland in the employ of Hama Tartus. Tartus had been a friend and co-worker of Felix Frage's and now he was buying the Hotel Kuckkuckuhr.

My chief interest during these years of captivity has been history, specifically the intriguing Schles-

wig-Holstein Question. Over the years, I am proud
to say, I have contributed in a small way to the distinguished body of literature on this Question, and
have become known, in a minor way, as an authority.
A few years ago a British journalist, Miss Joslyn
Frank, was given permission to visit me in order to
interview me on the Question. (As I understand it
she had some influence with Kurt Krauss himself.)
She was writing a book with the facetious title, *Who
Cares Who Killed Schleswig-Holstein?*, reflecting an
iconoclastic attitude which I deplore. Nevertheless I
found her a pleasant person, well-educated for a
woman.

The Schleswig-Holstein Question was responsible
for my next visitor, the young American writer,
Marty Hollands. Although he's primarily a writer of
crime fiction, he was interested in using the Question
as background material, and sought me out. Unable
to visit me in the usual way, this enterprising lad
disguised himself as a mailman, then as the water
meter-reader, the butcher's delivery boy, and the
plumber. Finally he persuaded me to let him help
us escape. Arriving in a dog-catcher's truck, he convinced the guards that a rabid dog had been seen
hiding under our porch. Ingrid and I donned fur coats
and crept into the back of the truck which Marty
Hollands then drove away.

In this undignified fashion we left Germany and
our long captivity, and only once on the drive south
toward Switzerland did I see our rescuer betray any
nervousness at all. Coming down through Bavaria,
we were stuck for quite a long while behind a large
and seedy circus, its trucks and wagons taking up
the small road, making it impossible for us to pass.

At the same time, a military staff car was directly behind us, also unable to pass, and full of German officers! I was afraid Marty's nervousness would give us away or cause an accident, but at last the road widened, the open staff car surged away from us with a roar, and we too could pass the circus, with the name "Rundelman's" on the sides of its vehicles. I remembered Rundelman's Circus from the old days, before our house arrest, when I would sometimes take Ingrid—just a child, then—to see it. I was surprised to find Rundelman's so far south; when I'd known the circus, it stayed very much in the north, near the sea.

Once in Switzerland, I directed Marty Hollands to bring us here, to the Hotel Kuckkuckuhr, where I knew kind Frau Freya Frage would shelter us. We arrived three days ago, and hope to make our way to America as soon as the mountain passes are cleared. It has not escaped my notice that young Hollands has a romantic interest in my little Ingrid; she, alas, is too distraught with suffering to reciprocate.

Besides Frau Freya Frage, there are three people here in the hotel whom I recognize from former days. First (I blush to tell the tale) is Mademoiselle Gelda Pourboire. Six years ago in Kiel, a colleague introduced us. I understood she had led a somewhat irregular life before then, but she told me she wanted to settle down, become a member of the *bourgeoisie*. Somehow or other I found myself in a rather passionate relationship with this beautiful woman. I even found myself wondering if she would become the mother my sweet Ingrid needed. But it didn't last, I sensed she was becoming restless, and then one day

she left me. Just as well for I don't think we were
truly compatible. I hope she is discreet for I would
be greatly embarrassed if the story got out.

I also recognize Leopold Schmendrick. He's a ship
designer, a nice chap, I knew him socially in the old
days in Kiel. I remember reading about Captain
Wilhelm Trehn a few years ago, also in Kiel. He was
a police officer then, who became caught up in a
notorious scandal. It was a protection racket, involv-
ing blackmail and extortion; an ugly business. Witnesses were afraid to testify so nothing could be
proved, but Trehn was fired. And now he's here and
I sense he's up to his old tricks. He wouldn't recognize
me as we never met, but I must say, the man terrifies
me. He could have us sent back to Germany!

I'd never met Hama Tartus before. He and Frau
Freya Frage obviously love one another, and have
assured me they will protect Ingrid and me. Miss
Olivia Quaile, Mr. Wayne Radford and Mr. Basil
Naunton, are all strangers to me. Which brings me
finally to Kurt Krauss.

For years I've thought of Herr Krauss as my worst
enemy, the one man responsible for all our suffering.
Imagine my feelings when Frau Frage whispered
that the grossly fat man who sat engorging himself
with food was the infamous Krauss! Ingrid and I
were carrying poison capsules to take in case we were
captured en route. As we passed Krauss's table, poor
Ingrid fainted, overcome by her emotions. At that
moment I emptied my capsule into Krauss's plate.
Some time later, as I was preparing for bed, Captain
Trehn arrived to announce that Herr Krauss was
dead.

I accept full responsibilty for my action about
which Ingrid knows nothing, nothing whatsoever.

Ingrid Diederich

I killed Kurt Krauss.

I am twenty years old, the only child of Professor Rudolf Diederich. My mother died long ago. I have very little experience of the world because for the last five years—that's a quarter of my lifetime—Papa and I have been confined to our house in Kiel, under house arrest. Papa used to be a famous scientist. He invented submarines (everyone's heard of the R-boat, the S-boat and the T-boat) and he had a chair at the University of Kiel. Then a very bad man named Kurt Krauss denounced poor Papa to the Nazis, I'm not really sure why.

For five years we couldn't leave the house, or have any visitors. I couldn't go to school. I didn't mind that too much because I wasn't much of a student, but I missed my friends. Poor Papa missed his work. He kept busy studying the Schleswig-Holstein Question, which is his hobby. It's something to do with history—I never got that far in school, so I couldn't tell you what it was all about.

For the first three years that we were under house arrest, Frau Freya Frage was with us, working as our housekeeper. Things weren't so bad then; she'd bring us news and gossip, and make sure we had nice things to eat. She was married to a seaman and he drowned. She was very upset after that, and not too long afterward she left Kiel to come here, to help Hama Tartus run the Hotel Kuckkuckuhr. (We didn't know Hama Tartus then. Frau Frage said he'd been a friend of her husband's.)

The next thing that happened was two months ago when a man named Marty Hollands came to the house disguised as a mailman because he wanted to talk with Papa about Schleswig-Holstein. He's American. He kept coming back, dressed up as the water meter-reader, and the plumber, and so on. Finally he talked Papa into letting him help us to escape. He pretended to be the dog-catcher and we put on fur coats and hid in his truck and he drove us away, toward Switzerland.

There was only one really scary moment on the drive down. We were on a narrow road in Bavaria, with a big slow-moving circus in front of us, and an open car full of German army officers right behind us. I could tell Marty was worried, but nothing happened, and as soon as the road widened the car behind us roared on by. Then we too passed the circus, and I saw its name—Rundelman's—and I remembered that when I was a little girl, Papa and I sometimes went to Rundelman's. I always liked it, but the last time we went there was a new midget in the circus that I didn't like at all. He was very bad-tempered, as though he thought he was too good for us, as though he didn't like everybody staring at him. But isn't that what midgets are for?

At last we arrived in Switzerland, and came straight here to this hotel. Papa wanted to come here because Frau Freya Frage is here, and she always said she wanted to help us. We've been here for three days and as soon as we can leave, Marty Hollands is going to take us to the United States of America, and Papa can get a job again. I'm not sure what I'll do—probably just look after dear Papa. I'm too old now to go to school, I think.

There are two women here that I think I've seen before. They sit together at dinner. Joslyn Frank came to the house once to interview Papa about the Schleswig-Holstein thing. And Gelda Pourboire visited us once a long time ago, I can't remember why. There were newspaper stories about Captain Trehn back in Kiel—he did something very bad, I don't know what. Everyone here seems to be afraid of him. Papa's worried that he could have us sent back to Germany.

Papa remembers Leopold Schmendrick from the old days but I don't. The others—Olivia Quaile, Wayne Radford, Basil Naunton—are all new to me. I don't pay much attention to what goes on in the hotel. All I can think about is the danger we are in.

When Papa and I realized that the fat man at the corner table was the evil Kurt Krauss we became very frightened. He seems to have some power over Hama Tartus. Poor Papa—what will become of him?

I could hardly eat dinner, I was so upset. When we left the table I pretended to faint near Kurt Krauss. I had a poison capsule in my pocket, to take in case the Gestapo caught us, and I quickly opened it and emptied it into Herr Krauss's food.

When Captain Trehn came to tell us Kurt Krauss was dead I was glad. I killed him all by myself—Papa had nothing to do with it.

Frau Freya Frage

I used to live in Kiel with my husband, Felix Frage, who was sometimes a seaman and sometimes a cook. Several years ago I learned he was also a spy for American Intelligence. Poor Felix lacked the nerve to lead a double life—he was a frightened man, always afraid something would catch up with him.

At that time I was working as housekeeper for Herr Professor Rudolf Diederich, a naval scientist at the University of Kiel. I became very fond of the Professor and his teenaged daughter, Ingrid. The Diederichs had been confined to their home, under house arrest, since the Nazis came to power in 1933, and I did what I could to brighten their dreary captivity.

Felix's best friend was another seaman, a Levantine named Hama Tartus. I liked Hama and I was glad when he and Felix got work on a private yacht, the Nilpferd, owned by the powerful critic, Kurt Krauss. Krauss liked to take his important friends out cruising in the North Sea.

On the third trip a terrible tragedy occurred. As Hama Tartus later told me, Felix had been drinking brandy alone late at night in the galley. Somehow he missed his footing and fell overboard and drowned. I've never been entirely satisfied with this story; I know Felix drank very little and avoided brandy because it gave him heartburn. I've always suspected his spying caught up with him. But I've never shared my doubts with anyone, not even Hama, who knows nothing about Felix's double life. In these difficult times the less you know, the safer you are.

Naturally I was terribly distressed at the loss of Felix. My only comfort was Hama Tartus who visited me often and tried to cheer me up. Gradually our friendship deepened into love. I am not the sort of woman who lives in sin—far from it—but because Felix's body was never recovered, Hama and I are not free to marry. I never would have consented to live with him openly in Kiel, but here in Switzerland it is different.

We came here several months after Felix drowned. Hama knew I wanted to start a new life with him, and he borrowed money from Kurt Krauss to buy this hotel. Our life here was serene and happy until Captain Wilhelm Trehn turned up. He's the local police officer, stationed in the village of Käseberg. He used to be in the police force in Kiel, where he was involved in a big scandal. He was the ringleader of a protection racket, and narrowly escaped prosecution.

In a smaller way he's doing the same thing here. Poor Hama Tartus has no passport—he's really a stateless person—which Captain Trehn quickly discovered. He's been squeezing us for money, threatening to have Hama deported if he doesn't pay up. Hama and I have been skimming money out of the hotel's profits, and now our silent partner, Kurt Krauss, is asking questions. He's had money troubles too, and he's pressuring Hama to repay the money he lent him. What would become of me without Hama Tartus? I'm so upset and worried that tonight when Kurt Krauss walked into the dining room I dropped the tray I was carrying.

As if things weren't bad enough, lately the hotel has been filling up with fugitives. The first was Leopold Schmendrick, who used to be a ship designer

before he had to flee Germany. He was helpful to
Hama in the old days, in Kiel, so naturally we were
glad to shelter him. But Captain Trehn spotted him
at once. Poor Leopold can't afford to bribe Trehn, so
it looks like he'll be sent back to Germany.

Then, three days ago, the Diederichs arrived, with
Marty Hollands, the young American writer. He
helped them to escape from the house in Kiel. He's
in love with Ingrid (a woman knows this sort of
thing), but the poor child is too mixed up to notice
him. So far Trehn hasn't made any moves against
the Diederichs, but it's only a matter of time.

As for the other guests here, I do seem to recall
seeing Olivia Quaile once, years ago. Felix knew her;
she was a retired governess who had befriended him
because she was assembling fish recipes for a cookbook. I guess she's still at it, because she's asked me
for recipes since she came here. She also asked me
about some circus she thought was going to appear
near here, that I knew nothing about; poor thing, I
suppose she's moving into second childhood.

The other guests—Gelda Pourboire, Joslyn Frank,
Wayne Radford and Basil Naunton—are all new to
me.

Tonight all the guests had left the dining room,
but Kurt Krauss remained, still eating. How that
man could eat! I came back into the room to see if
he wanted more pudding, only to find him dead, face
down in the tapioca. What a shock! For once I was
glad Captain Trehn was here, in the Hotel Kuckkuckuhr.

Hama Tartus

I am a stateless person, born somewhere along the eastern shore of the Mediterranean, orphaned young, part of the human flotsam and jetsam of these troubled times. I was a seaman in my youth. Several years ago, on a foul tramp steamer with an alcohol-sodden wreck of a captain, I jumped ship at Kiel, Germany. There I was able to pick up menial labor around the docks, and hoped eventually to find a better life for myself.

A seacook named Felix Frage befriended me, and brought me home to meet his wife, Freya. Felix was a jumpy sort of fellow, always looking over his shoulder, so to speak. Through Felix I found jobs on boats out of Kiel and eventually landed work on the Nilpferd, a new yacht owned by a great whale of a man named Kurt Krauss. He was a cruel master, widely hated, but I make it a policy to get along with everyone, so I had no trouble with him. Krauss's lady friend at that time was a French *chanteuse* named Gelda Pourboire. Their's was a stormy relationship, full of *Sturm und Drang*. One particularly tempestuous night Gelda made her way to my bunk and we made love. That was on the first cruise.

On the third cruise there was a tragic—event. One night I was awakened by the sound of a thud. I went to the galley where I found Felix dead, and Krauss standing over him with an iron skillet. Krauss told me he had learned that Felix was a spy, in the pay of U.S. intelligence, and that when confronted, Felix had attacked him with a cleaver, forcing Krauss to kill him in self defense. Krauss didn't want any of this story to get out and he asked me to help him cover it up. Together we weighted the body with canned goods and pans and pushed it overboard. I left an empty brandy bottle on the galley floor to suggest that Felix had gotten drunk and fallen overboard.

Among the guests aboard on that cruise were three people who are now staying at the Kuckkuckuhr: Besides Gelda they were Wayne Radford and Basil Naunton, those two sportsmen, who had business dealings with Kurt Krauss, I believe.

Immediately after Felix's disappearance the Nilpferd returned to port and I testified at the official investigation. The verdict was accidental drowning. Freya was naturally very upset, and suspicious, but I never told her or anyone else what had actually happened. I visited her often and we gradually became quite close. Unfortunately we cannot marry, as Felix's body was never found. A few months after the event I went to Kurt Krauss to say that I no longer wished to go to sea, and that I'd saved a little money over the years and wanted to establish myself in business. Krauss volunteered to assist me as long as I left Germany. This is how Freya and I came to buy the Hotel Kuckkuckuhr, with Kurt Krauss as our not-so-silent partner.

(I know this may sound to overscrupulous ears like blackmail, or even like some sort of betrayal of my friend Felix. I don't see it this way. Nothing I could have done would have brought Felix back to life. I made the best of a bad situation. Life has taught me to be a pragmatist.)

Not long after we came here Krauss told me he'd had some serious financial reverses and he wished he hadn't given me so much money. I told him I'd repay it as soon as possible. This won't be as easy as it seems. Unfortunately my papers—which are no better than clumsy forgeries—have been seen through by the local policeman, Captain Wilhelm Trehn. I remembered him from Kiel, where he used to be on the police force. He and his fellow officers were caught in a notorious protection racket and he had to leave. And now he's up to his old tricks, extorting money from people like myself. He threatens to have me deported if I don't pay up. To satisfy him I'm reduced to skimming profits from this hotel, which I'm terrified Krauss will discover. Between Captain Trehn and Kurt Krauss I'm in a bad way. Poor Freya has also suffered. Her nerves have never recovered from Felix's death. She's terrified Kurt Krauss will learn of my embezzling and will make trouble for us, as he has done for so many others. Last night when Krauss entered the dining room she was so frightened she dropped the tray she was carrying.

In the midst of all our other troubles, who should show up but Leopold Schmendrick, seeking shelter. I knew him also in Kiel. He was a ship designer, and he helped me out once or twice, finding me odd jobs. Now he's running from the Gestapo, hasn't got a passport, and Captain Trehn is determined to deport him. It's unfortunate but there's no way I can help. Professor Diederich and his daughter, Ingrid, are another couple of refugees. Freya used to work for them in Kiel and they were always very kind to her, so naturally they came here when they escaped from Germany. So far they've avoided Captain Trehn's attentions.

I've also met Olivia Quaile, the old American lady,

before. Felix Frage knew her, oddly enough, and he once told me she was collecting recipes for a fish cookbook. The other guests—Joslyn Frank and Marty Hollands—are strangers to me.

Tonight after most of the guests had left the dining room, Captain Trehn put the collar on poor Schmendrick and locked him up in his room. I was in the kitchen washing up when I heard Freya scream. She had found Kurt Krauss, dead in his pudding. It was she who told Captain Trehn.

Leopold Schmendrick

I killed Kurt Krauss.

I am a ship's architect from Kiel. I was active politically during the years of the Weimar Republic; a fact that has recently been blown up way out of proportion. All I've ever wanted was to be allowed to do my work—designing yachts—in peace.

When the Nazis came to power there was less need for civilian boats and more for military ships. I never had a high security clearance so I didn't work on secret projects, but I did do some work for the German Navy, as well as continuing with the few private commissions that came along.

Three years ago I designed and oversaw the construction of a yacht, the Nilpferd, for Herr Kurt Krauss, at the Elbe River shipyard at Hamburg. I was never paid. Finally, after dunning him unsuccessfully for years, I commenced legal action. Suddenly the Gestapo was after me. I—a lifelong liberal—was accused of being a communist! From a friend I learned that Kurt Krauss was the source of this false accusation. Evidently Krauss had suffered financial reversals and was unable to meet his obligations, and so had taken the expedient of denouncing me. The swine!

The Gestapo had taken my passport and I knew it was only a matter of hours before they took me, so I fled. I made my way to the Hotel Kuckkuckuhr, where I knew Hama Tartus would give me shelter. He had been a seaman in Kiel, and I had helped him find work on occasion and he was grateful. I've been here for a week. Hama Tartus and Frau Freya Frage

Leopold Schmendrick at the end of his rope.

(they are not married but they live together as man and wife) have been very kind to me, but I don't feel safe. That policeman, Captain Wilhelm Trehn, has his eye on me. Although I didn't know him at the time, he used to be a policeman in Kiel, where he was involved in an ugly scandal about a protection racket. I think he's got something on Hama Tartus—I know Tartus fears him almost as much as I do. I have no money at all, I can't pay protection, and I have nowhere to go but here.

When I came into the dining room tonight and saw my enemy, Kurt Krauss, I was so startled I stumbled against his chair, spilling his beer. On a lightning impulse I took the poison capsule that I have kept in my pocket since my troubles began, and dropped it into his glass. Better him than me!

Hama Tartus led me away, seating me with the old American lady, Olivia Quaile. This sweet old soul was kind enough to try to distract me from my worries during dinner. A retired governess, she keeps herself busy amassing recipes for a cookbook. She was very interested in my work, and quite knowledgeable about the German coast and the various shipyards.

In the course of the evening (while I kept an eye on Kurt Krauss, waiting for the poison to take effect), I noticed several familiar faces in the dining room. I met Gelda Pourboire several years ago when she was Kurt Krauss's mistress. One night, to my astonishment, this beauteous and sophisticated creature indicated that she found me—me! little Leopold Schmendrick!—not entirely unattractive. One thing led to another, and the upshot of it was that I enjoyed her most enjoyable favors, on a bunk on the as yet uncompleted Nilpferd.

I also recognized Professor Rudolf Diederich and his young daughter, Ingrid. He used to be a naval scientist at the University of Kiel, so our social circles overlapped. I believe he's been under house arrest for several years. And I met Joslyn Frank with Kurt Krauss while I was working on the Nilpferd. She's a British journalist who subsequently wrote a highly unflattering magazine article about him. Marty Hollands, Wayne Radford and Basil Naunton were all new faces to me.

Mostly though, I watched Captain Trehn. I knew he was going to arrest me. I saw Hama Tartus speak to him, in a vain appeal to try to save me. Trehn knows I have no money, I'm not a candidate for a shakedown. Having me sent back to Germany will demonstrate to other unfortunates what fate awaits those who can't bribe Wilhelm Trehn.

Only Krauss remained in the dining room when Trehn made his move. Hama Tartus and Frau Freya Frage watched with sadness and sympathy as the policeman led me away, past Kurt Krauss, that arch-fiend. He locked me up in my room, planning to take me away in the morning.

When Trehn told me Kurt Krauss had been killed I saw no reason not to admit having poisoned him. What can I possibly lose now?

Olivia Quaile

I killed Kurt Krauss.

I'm retired now, after working many years as a governess. I know you wouldn't think it to look at me but I've been just about everywhere, teaching the children of diplomats and foreign service officers. You may have heard of my brother, Quentin Quaile; he's now head of the American Secret Service and has been in intelligence work all his life. He was often influential in arranging for me to be employed in one place or another. And of course I was always happy to gather whatever information would be useful to dear Quentin and our dear country. In a modest way I was able to be rather useful on quite a few occasions. People don't much notice a little old lady, so it's easy for me to go places and find things out. (I don't like that word, "spy".) And people tell me things that they might not tell someone who seemed important.

For the last few years, since I've retired, I've been collecting recipes for a fish cookbook. This engrossing project has taken me all over Europe, to France and Russia and England, and of course Germany. It was in Kiel that I met Felix Frage, a few years ago. He was a seacook, so naturally he had all sorts of ideas about cooking fish. And he'd been in the employ of the American Secret Service for several years. Poor Felix was not naturally gifted at intelligence work. He had a haunted, furtive look that made him look as if he had a secret. When I heard that he had fallen overboard while working on Kurt Krauss's yacht, the Nilpferd, I strongly suspected that Krauss had found him out and eliminated him. It was well known that Krauss was an important Nazi.

Miss Olivia Quaile explains her role in all this.

Recently I've spent several weeks at the Hotel Splendide, in Kiel. I've passed the time quite pleasantly collecting recipes in the various coastal villages. And in my travels I've kept my eyes and ears open. Our government was very curious to know the whereabouts of Germany's new secret submarine base. It took me almost two months but I finally found it, I'm proud to say.

During my stay in Kiel I became acquainted with a British journalist, Joslyn Frank. We first met over lunch in a small *Gasthaus* on the coast, where I had gone in my search for recipes. Two English speaking ladies, traveling alone, with similar interests (she's a journalist, assigned to uncover evidence of the German naval buildup along the Baltic); we quite naturally struck up a conversation. And as Joslyn had a car I found it convenient to travel with her. She also served as protective coloration. A few days ago her visa was suddenly revoked and she was forced to leave Germany. My work was ended and I was heading here, so I suggested she accompany me. She was kind enough to drive me here in her car.

My reason for coming here, to the Hotel Kuckkuckuhr, was that I was supposed to meet my contact and pass along the information about the location of the secret German submarine base. More than that I cannot divulge—no, not even if you torture me. All I can say is that I have not yet passed on the information.

Last night before dinner in the sitting room, I encountered three men whose acquaintance I had made in Kiel, at the Hotel Splendide. They were Marty Hollands, a young American writer of thrillers (I must confess that I love to read these books—it is my worst vice), and two gentlemen who were traveling together, Wayne Radford and Basil Naunton. (There's something a bit *shady* about those two, don't you agree?) Radford and Naunton told a lengthy and, to my mind, tasteless, anecdote about an incident they'd witnessed en route. A midget traveling with a circus had been arrested by the Gestapo. I realized that this must be the circus I'd been looking forward to attending, as it was supposed to be playing in this area just around now, and I do love circuses. Ah, well.

Later, during dinner, I showed Radford and Naunton my map and asked them to point out exactly where this incident had taken place, just in case it was something my superiors would need to know about.

During dinner I sat with Leopold Schmendrick, whom I had not met before, and this poor unfortunate man told me his sad story. There were other people in the dining room, in addition to those I have already mentioned: Our hosts, Hama Tartus and Frau Freya Frage, widow of the unfortunate Felix; Professor Rudolf Diederich and his young daughter, Ingrid; the glamorous Frenchwoman, Gelda Pourboire; the local policeman, Captain Wilhelm Trehn. And there was Kurt Krauss.

How and why did I kill Kurt Krauss? The man is an enemy to America. Not to mention an offense to good taste. Look at all the wickedness this one person has generated: Poor Leopold Schmendrick, hounded out of Germany. Felix Frage, killed. Joslyn Frank, her visa revoked. And much more and worse, I'm sure. Looking at the faces of the kind people about me I could see their fear of this monstrous man. Frau Freya Frage dropped her tray when he entered the room.

So I killed him. And how did I accomplish this?
Easily. I always carry a tiny vial of poison in my
reticule, disguised as lavender scent. Pretending to
wish to talk with Herr Krauss about my travels, I
waved my map under his nose. Under cover of the
paper I swiftly opened the vial and dumped its con-
tents on his sauerkraut.

After dinner I retired to my room where I waited
calmly for the news. Switzerland is, I know, a
civilized country. I trust this comic opera policeman,
Captain Trehn, will do his part: Take me into custody
and contact my attorney, Ulysses Schönberg. Quentin will know how to find him.

Joslyn Frank answers questions for a change.

Joslyn Frank

I am a journalist, of British nationality. I first met Kurt Krauss three years ago. I was on assignment from an English magazine to write an article about him and I spent some months in Germany, following him about and asking him questions and finding out what I could. (I was also, at the same time, researching a book I later wrote, *Who Cares Who Killed Schleswig-Holstein?*, but that's another story.) Eventually my article, *The Most Hated Man In Hamburg*, was published. If I do say so myself, the piece presented a fair and accurate picture of the loathesome fat bully. Needless to say he didn't like it, and he retaliated by getting right-wing toadies in London (of which, alas, there are many) to have me blackballed out of most of my British markets. Which is why I'm now working for *American Mercury*.

My current assignment is two-fold. While my cover is a series of innocuous travel articles about the delights of northern Germany, in fact I'm seeking out evidence of the Nazi arms build-up, particularly the massive increase in the German Navy, including submarines. I've heard rumors of a new submarine manufacturing facility somewhere along the Baltic Coast but I haven't found it. I just spent a month in the area, based in Kiel, driving all along the coast. One day at lunch in a *Gasthaus* in the town of Schönberg I struck up an acquaintance with a little old American lady named Olivia Quaile, a retired nanny. She's "a writer too" as she never stops telling me—she's collecting recipes for a fish cookbook, and was determined to scour every inch of the north German coast

71

to unearth recipes. She's a bit balmy but I don't mind her, and I find her useful as protective coloration, so we've been traveling together.

Recently my old friend Kurt Krauss found out I was back in Germany, and used his influence to have my visa revoked. I was sorry to have to leave before I'd located the submarine base, but I was given twenty-four hours. Miss Quaile—I guess she's finally completed her recipe collection—was also leaving, heading here to the Hotel Kuckkuckuhr, so I volunteered to drive her. The choice of hotel was hers.

We arrived here yesterday, and would have been on our way to Italy today but for the snow storm. There are several people here whom I've met before in the course of my travels. I met Professor Rudulf Diederich, and his rather dim-witted daughter, Ingrid, two years ago, while I was working on the Schleswig-Holstein book. He's an amateur historian, something of an authority (and a bit of a crank) on the Schleswig-Holstein Question, and I wanted to interview him. I learned that he was being held under house arrest and wasn't allowed to have visitors. I got around that problem with the help of Kurt Krauss, who obtained the necessary permission for me. He was eager to please me then because I was working on my article about him, and he hoped I'd paint him in a favorable light. Was he disappointed!

Anyway, I met with Professor Diederich and we had a fruitful discussion, although he disagreed entirely with my thesis. (Briefly, my book presents the argument that disputes of historical right and wrong are irrelevant, reality supersedes morality. Using the Schleswig-Holstein Question as *reductio ad absurdum,* I demonstrated that there is no absolutely correct answer to the Question—events create their own solution. Besides which, I personally find the notion that a royal succession cannot pass through the female line, being the situation in one answer to the Question, morally repugnant.)

Last night, entering the dining room, I encountered Gelda Pourboire, a French nightclub singer whom I met in Germany a few years ago. At that time she and Kurt Krauss were having a rather stormy affair; I wasn't at all surprised last night to learn that it had ended. She suggested we sit together and I jumped at the idea, having had quite enough of Olivia Quaile's chatter. Gelda and I had a good gossip, mostly about Krauss, but I didn't learn anything I didn't already know.

There was one other person at the Hotel Kuckkuckuhr whom I recognized: Leopold Schmendrick. He's a ship designer, who seems to have fallen on evil days. When I knew him he was designing a yacht for Herr Krauss. Now Gelda tells me Krauss claims to have designed it himself.

Although I'd not met him, Marty Hollands and I had corresponded. He wrote to me about my book, *Who Cares Who Killed Schleswig-Holstein?* He's a thriller writer.

Captain Wilhelm Trehn's name was familiar to me. A few years ago he was involved in a scandal in Kiel. He and some other policemen there had a protective racket going—extorting money from the local sinners. And now he's here in Switzerland, and by the way he's throwing his considerable weight around, I'd guess he's up to his old tricks.

The others here—Hama Tartus, Frau Frage, Wayne Radford and Basil Naunton—are strangers to me.

When I saw Kurt Krauss in the dining room last night, busily stuffing food into that fat face, I went over and told him just what I thought of him. I half-hoped to provoke him into saying or doing something newsworthy (it's a journalistic technique that often works) but he just waved me away. Gelda Pourboire took my rebuff personally and went over to give Kurt Krauss a piece of her mind and he was just as disagreeable to her.

After dinner, Gelda and I were having coffee in the sitting room when Captain Trehn told us Krauss had dropped dead. Well, it's not the story I started out to write, but it'll have to do!

Gelda Pourboire

I am an *artiste,* French by birth, and I have appeared in theatres and nightclubs and films throughout Europe. I sing, I dance, I perform. It is true, I have had many lovers. Men admire me, they flock around me like moths about the flame . . .

Six years ago I was in Kiel, in Germany, where I met a widower named Herr Professor Rudolf Diederich. It was a moment when I was feeling a bit *fatiguée.* I thought I might quiet down, settle down, slow down, and the Professor was such a nice and decent man. We had an affair. He even introduced me to his teenaged daughter, Ingrid. He was nice but *mon dieu!,* was he dull. He cured me of wanting to slow down, let me tell you.

Two years after that, back in Kiel again, I took up with a very different sort of fellow, Captain Wilhelm Trehn. Willy was a cop, as crooked as they come. He liked to boast about how everyone was terrified of him because he had the goods on them. He took me around his office, showed me all his weapons and souvenirs, vials of poison from famous murder cases. Men are all the same, they love to show off.

It was Willy who introduced me to Kurt Krauss, at a party at Krauss's big house on the Elbe River, near Hamburg. That was three years ago. The man was grossly fat, like a mountain, *dégoutant.* Still, I could see he was attracted to me, and I hoped he would help me in my career because he was a very important person in theatre and cinema in Germany, so . . .

Gelda Pourboire wants everyone to know she's a good girl.

We were together, Krauss and I, for a year. We quarreled all the time. He was using me, that pig of a man! He never lifted a finger to help me, never gave me a role in any of his films. I had no reason to be true to him, and I wasn't.

Leopold Schmendrick was the first. He was a ship's architect and he was working on Krauss's new yacht, the Nilpferd. He was sweet, not very experienced with women. One night he let me come aboard the Nilpferd while it was still in the shipyard and one thing led to another . . .

Of course Krauss had to go to the Berlin Olympics in 1936 and I went with him (what a bore!), and that's where I met those two sportsmen, Wayne Radford and Basil Naunton. Nice fellows. I spent a night with Wayne and then a night with Basil—or maybe it was the other way around.

After the Olympics the Nilpferd was ready to sail and Krauss took me along on several cruises. I hate the sea, but I managed to amuse myself. On the first trip I spent an evening with Hama Tartus, who was a member of the crew. (He's come up in the world since then, he's now running the Hotel Kuckkuc-kuhr.) The Nilpferd's cook, Felix Frage, helped me pass the time on the second cruise.

The third cruise was cut short by an unpleasant incident. Felix Frage got drunk one night and fell overboard and drowned—or so it was said. No one saw it happen and the body was never recovered. Wayne Radford and Basil Naunton were also on the Nilpferd for that trip. They had some sort of business dealings with Kurt Krauss, I believe.

Not long after that last cruise my affair with Kurt Krauss came to an end. The man was impossible to live with. He had never been what you would call *gentil,* and then around this time he had some sort of financial *débacle* (I don't know about these things, so don't ask me), and he became a monster. He had given some money to Hama Tartus (perhaps the money he used to finance this hotel), and he kept saying he wished he still had it. He had big debts and no money to pay them.

Unfortunately, around this time Krauss discovered that I had been signing his name on some checks. I needed money to buy clothes, lingerie, shoes; the things a girl must have. When he found out he exploded. He had me arrested and I was sent to jail! I served six months before one of my admirers, a lawyer, helped me to get freed. That was a terrible experience, let me tell you.

I got out of jail a year and a half ago. I've worked on and off, mostly in France. Recently I was offered a permanent engagement in a nightclub in Kiel. On the train from France to Germany I met Marty Hollands, the young American writer who is staying here at the Kuckkuckuhr. Such a charming boy! We spent a delightful evening together (I won't spell it out), then went our separate ways.

The job in Kiel lasted only two months. One night Kurt Krauss was in the audience, in a group of German businessmen. The next day the owner of the club told me he had to let me go. At first he wouldn't say why but I persuaded him to admit the truth—Kurt Krauss, my *bête noire,* had pressured the man to have me fired. I was furious. I went to Krauss's house in Hamburg to have it out with him but the servants wouldn't let me in. Once I cooled off I decided to get out of Germany. I arrived here yesterday, and

I wasn't at all pleased to see Krauss. If it weren't for all this snow I would have left today. I have no interest in resuming relations with any of the men here—with me, once it's ended, that's it; *fini*.

As for the rest of the people here, I've never met Olivia Quaile or Frau Freya Frage before. I have met Joslyn Frank. Two years ago she interviewed Kurt Krauss for an article she was writing for a British magazine. I remember when it was published it made him very angry. I was glad to see Joslyn again last night. We shared a table and had a good talk. Kurt Krauss's ears must have been burning! I would not have bothered to say anything to him, but after he was so rude to Joslyn Frank I had to. I told him exactly what I thought of him, I'm happy to say. Joslyn and I left the table together. We were having coffee in the sitting room when Captain Trehn appeared to tell us Herr Krauss was dead. Oo la la!

Radford and Naunton have a land deal you might be interested in.

Wayne Radford &
Basil Naunton

We're a team, a pair of lucky chaps—one from Kent, one from Pennsylvania—who don't have to work for a living. Gentlemen of leisure, we're free to travel the world, following our consuming interest, which is sports. Hunting, fishing, riding, you name it. Spectator sports—watching cricket matches or tennis matches or football games—fill our idler hours. What a life!

In fact, to be absolutely scout's honor truthful, we're not the simple sportsmen we seem. The Everglade Land Company (prospectus on request!) is our name, and swindling suckers is our game. Here's how it works: When we meet a mark we explain that we owe all our good fortune to our investments in Florida real estate. Participants make a hefty one-time investment, and are guaranteed a nice monthly income forever after. Well, they get their income for the first year (we use sucker B's money to pay sucker A's dividends), then they receive a letter from the Everglade Land Company announcing a reorganization, and that's the end of it. Since our prospects are all European and the mythical company is in Florida, once the checks stop coming in there's not much the marks can do about it. And so far as they know we two are fellow victims. Pretty sweet scam, what?

Two years ago we met Kurt Krauss at the '36 Olympics in Berlin, where we fleeced him well—ninety thousand U.S. dollars. Krauss could have gotten into deep trouble with the Nazis for exporting so much currency out of Germany, but his greed was greater than his patriotism. A year or so later when he realized he'd been rooked, he didn't dare go to the German police.

Kurt Krauss was then traveling with a French nightclub singer named Gelda Pourboire. *Femme fatale* type, don't you know? Gelda had a roving eye, and we both—separately—enjoyed her favors. We hadn't seen her since, and weren't sure at first that we recognized her last night; looked like her nose was out of joint, didn't she?

Around that time Krauss invited us for a cruise of the North Sea on his new yacht, the Nilpferd, which he told us he'd designed himself. Gelda Pourboire was still with him but they quarreled night and day. She wanted him to help her with her career but he wouldn't come through.

There's someone else here at the Kuckkuchuhr who seems familiar from that yacht trip, and that's our nervous host, the wily Levantine, Hama Tartus. We're both sure he was a member of the crew on the Nilpferd. We've never met the waitress Frau Freya Frage, before, but the name rings a bell. There was a cook on the yacht named Felix Frage, a nosy fellow who kept asking questions about ship-building on the north German coast. He asked us not to tell Krauss about his conversations with us: "He doesn't like us to fraternize with the guests." He was a furtive chap, slunk about looking over his shoulder. Then one day he disappeared, presumably having fallen overboard the night before. There was an empty brandy bottle in the galley and Krauss declared that Frage had gotten drunk and missed his step. No way of proving anything. That ended the cruise. We all went back to Hamburg where we were just as pleased to say *auf wiedersehen* to Herr Krauss.

That was the last time we saw him until last night. We knew he must have discovered by now that his $90,000 was gone forever, and we were curious to know if he would blame us. But we approached him boldly, full of manly confidence (we *are* confidence men, after all), offering to shake hands. He shooed us off rudely, his usual boorish self. It's hard to tell whether or not he held us responsible for his losses. We're not going to lose any sleep over it.

Before coming here we spent several weeks in Kiel, Germany, staying at the Hotel Splendide. Two of our fellow guests at the Kuckkuckuhr were also staying there, they being the young American writer, Marty Hollands, and the little old lady, Olivia Quaile. We'd struck a bit of an acquaintance with Hollands, over drinks in the Splendide bar—to the extent of learning that he lacked the wherewithal to become an Everglade's investor. Miss Quaile was a garrulous old bird, full of nosy questions. We learned to avoid her. And this British journalist, Joslyn Frank, was also in Kiel, although she wasn't staying at the same hotel. We used to see her and Olivia Quaile driving about town.

As for the others here, we don't know Leopold Schmendrick nor the Diederichs, father and daughter. The only other party we've had dealings with is that policeman, Captain Wilhelm Trehn. We went to see him the day before yesterday, before the snowstorm, in his office in Käseberg down in the valley. We asked about the prospect of deer hunting around these parts, and the man promptly hit us up for a bribe! Failed of course.

Before dinner last evening we renewed our acquaintance with Marty Hollands and Miss Quaile. We entertained them with the story of a peculiar incident we'd witnessed en route between Kiel and here. A traveling circus—rather a fleabag outfit, "Rundelman's" was the name on the wagons—had been stopped by the police. We watched as they searched all the trucks and wagons and finally found the man they were looking for—the midget! We two thought this was pretty amusing, but Hollands and Miss Quaile acted like we'd told a dirty joke in mixed company. Later during dinner, little Miss Quaile pestered us to show her on her map where the incident had taken place, and we obliged.

Otherwise the evening passed uneventfully until Captain Trehn roused us with the news that Kurt Krauss was dead. Bad business. Hope they get it cleared up soon so we can leave. We're on our way to the Italian Riviera where we hope to snag some new investors. We would have left yesterday except for the snow.

Captain Wilhelm Trehn

Achtung! I am a person of considerable influence and power in this neck of the mountains. I am captain of police of Käseberg, in the valley below the Hotel Kuckkuckuhr. Once upon a time I was a police office in Kiel, Germany. Those were the days, my friend. I had a finger in every pie in Kiel; I knew everyone worth knowing, and was feared by most of them. Kurt Krauss, the influential critic and producer, was my friend—he called me Willy. He used to invite me to parties at his estate near Hamburg, and he told all his important friends that I was his pet crook.

Four years ago I had an affair with Gelda Pourboire, the French nightclub singer, who was then appearing in a club in Kiel. We had been together for a few months, and it was already beginning to cool off when I took her to a party at Kurt Krauss's house. She was very eager to meet him because she knew he was a big name in show business and she thought he would help her with her career. I wasn't very surprised when she left me for Krauss. (As *mein* papa often said, "All women are whores.") I didn't see much of them after that. I heard that it was a stormy relationship; he never did anything to help her career (just between us, her talents lay in the bedroom, not on the stage), she was widely unfaithful to him, and eventually he threw her out when he caught her stealing from him. She may have even gone to jail because of this—I wouldn't know because I had to leave Kiel myself around that time.

For some time I and my colleagues in the police department had been running quite a lucrative business on the side. Protection was the name of our

Captain Wilhelm Trehn, no stranger to interrogation, parries the questions.

game. There were a lot of people in Kiel in 1935 who
were happy to pay well to keep out of trouble. Unfortunately one of my men was indiscreet, the au-
thorities got wind of what we were up to, and eventually the whole thing exploded in our faces. I was
lucky to get out of it without an indictment (I saw
to it that no witnesses testified), but I lost my job
and was forced to leave Germany. This is how I came
to this unimportant little corner of this ludicrous
little country.

However I soon discovered that even here there
was scope for my talents, Hama Tartus, who runs
the Hotel Kuckkuckuhr, became my first—shall we
say, client?—in this country. He is stateless, traveling with a pathetic forgery of a passport. The Swiss
don't like this sort of thing and would deport him if
they knew. But they don't know because I'm happy
to protect Herr Tartus, for a price. I also looked into
the background of his companion, Frau Freya Frage.
She comes from my hometown of Kiel; she's the
widow of Felix Frage, a cook who drowned while
drunk when he fell off Kurt Krauss's yacht, the
Nilpferd, two years ago, just before Tartus bought
this hotel. Interesting, but not enough to go on.

I have learned also that Kurt Krauss is a co-owner
of this hotel, having backed Tartus when he bought
it. I've heard from various sources that Krauss has
suffered financial reverses in recent years. Lately
he's been leaning hard on Tartus for repayment of
the money owed him. He's begun to look more closely
at the hotel's books and is convinced someone is embezzling. Today he told me he was going to track
down the thief and expose him. I tried to disuade
him, to convince him the hotel was losing money

because tourism is off this year, but he wouldn't listen. He even began to wonder if I was involved. Which I am, in a way—Hama Tartus is the embezzler, of course, and the money is going directly to my pocket.

Police work is just one headache after another. There's a circus due to arrive in Käseberg any day now; Rundelman's Circus, a German outfit. Everyone knows how much trouble that means—pickpockets and two-bit whores and all the usual riffraff, disrupting the local citizenry. As if I didn't have enough to worry about.

Another matter on my mind lately is one Leopold Schmendrick. These days Switzerland is lousy with people like him, fugitives from Germany. I soak them for whatever the traffic will bear. From time to time, if someone can't pay off I send them back—it makes my record look good, and it convinces the other refugees that I mean business. Schmendrick doesn't have a *pfennig,* so back to the *Vaterland* he goes. Tartus and his woman tried to persuade me to leave him alone, but I was firm. What kind of policeman would I be if I allowed myself to be swayed by pity?

There were several new faces in the dining room last night. The American writer, Marty Hollands, and Professor Diederich and his daughter, Ingrid, are traveling together. I suspect the Diederichs are potential customers. I'll look into that tomorrow; they're not going anywhere with all this snow. Joslyn Frank, the British journalist, and the foolish old lady, Olivia Quaile, are strangers to me.

Those two alleged sportsmen, Wayne Radford and Basil Naunton, came to my office in Käseberg the day before yesterday, to ask about deer hunting. I suggested a modest honorarium for my trouble, an idea they rudely rejected. There's something *ersatz* about those two—I'll keep my eye on them.

Last night when I entered the dining room I tried to have a word with Kurt Krauss. I wanted to let him know that I was working on the suspected embezzlement. He was busy eating and he dismissed me.

Frau Frage seated me with Hollands and we exchanged superficial pleasantries. It did not escape my notice that young Hollands was quite enamored of the Diederich *fraulein*—a tasty little morsel indeed. Mostly I watched Schmendrick. After all the diners except Krauss had left I made my move. It was while I was upstairs, locking Leopold Schmendrick in his room, that Kurt Krauss died. Frau Frage found the body and immediately summoned me.

I examined Krauss. His body was still warm, covered with tapioca pudding. It is my opinion that he was poisoned, and it is my further opinion that the poison might have been z-100, a lethal substance developed in 1933 by our brilliant German scientists. It is colorless, tasteless, quick-acting. The only evidence of its presence is a faint and not unpleasant odor of lavender. A similar though not identical scent was faintly noticeable on the body. I speak with some authority on this subject because, while I was on the police force in Kiel, I was given a small vial of z-100 to study. I passed many amusing hours experimenting with its effects upon small furry creatures, and when I left Germany I took the vial as a souvenir.

It is now my tedious duty to uncover the killer of Kurt Krauss. I have no doubt that I will succeed in this task. My greatest talent as a law enforcement officer is my unerring ability to detect wrongdoers—I can smell the presence of guilt. In this case my task has been complicated by the fact that no less than *five* guests at the hotel have confessed to the murder of Kurt Krauss. Really, a truer thing was never said than this: "A policeman's lot is not a happy one!"

The Quiz

Now that you've read this far, you've probably formed some strong impressions of what really happened at the Hotel Kuckkuckuhr. Take this quiz to see how well you're doing.

I. Matching

Match the names in the first column with the descriptions in the second column.

1. Marty Hollands
2. Olivia Quaile
3. Professor Diederich
4. Ingrid Diederich
5. Gelda Pourboire
6. Hama Tartus
7. Freya Frage
8. Captain Trehn
9. Wayne Radford &
   Basil Naunton
10. Leopold Schmendrick
11. Joslyn Frank

a. History-buff
b. Official
c. Butter-fingers
d. Faint-hearted
e. Leisured
f. Mercurial
g. Pragmatist
h. Liberal
i. Fish-disher
j. Dog-catcher
k. Artistic

II. Multiple Choice

Check one

1. Where did Wayne Radford and Basil Naunton
   first meet Gelda Pourboire?
   a. On the yacht, the Nilpferd
   b. On a train
   c. At the 1936 Berlin Olympics
   d. In Kiel

2. What was the connection between Felix Frage
   and Captain Trehn?
   a. Trehn killed Felix
   b. Trehn blackmailed Felix
   c. They were both spies for the USA
   d. None

3. Why was Professor Diederich held under house
   arrest?
   a. Because of his liberal political views
   b. Because Kurt Krauss wanted to place a friend
      of his in his univeristy post
   c. Because he refused to pay protection to Captain
      Trehn
   d. Because he wouldn't design submarines for the
      Nazis

4. Why did the affair between Kurt Krauss and
   Gelda Pourboire come to an end?
   a. He wouldn't give her a part in a movie
   b. He caught her stealing from him
   c. He discovered she was unfaithful to him
   d. She got tired of him

5. What was Marty Hollands's beef against Kurt Krauss?
   a. Krauss owed him money
   b. Krauss had a yen for Ingrid
   c. They disagreed on the Schleswig-Holstein Question
   d. They had opposing political views

6. What was the title of Joslyn Frank's magazine article?
   a. *The Beast of Bremerhaven*
   b. *Stain on the Pedigree*
   c. *Who Cares Who Killed Schleswig-Holstein?*
   d. *The Most Hated Man in Hamburg*

7. Which of these travellers did *not* see Rundelman's Circus while en route from Germany to Switzerland?
   a. Wayne Radford & Basil Naunton
   b. Professor and Ingrid Diederich
   c. Joslyn Frank and Olivia Quaile
   d. Marty Hollands

8. Why is Captain Trehn hounding Leopold Schmendrick?
   a. Kurt Krauss told him to do so
   b. Schmendrick has no money to bribe Trehn
   c. Trehn is convinced he's a spy
   d. Trehn needs a scapegoat for Krauss's murder

9. What is the link between Freya Frage and Olivia Quaile?
   a. They are both working for U.S. Intelligence
   b. They met on the Nilpferd, through Kurt Krauss
   c. They met on the Nilpferd, through Felix Frage
   d. Olivia Quaile has talked with Freya Frage about her recipes

10. What is Hama Tartus most afraid of?
   a. That Captain Trehn will have him deported
   b. That Freya Frage will learn of his role in Felix's death
   c. That Kurt Krauss will denounce him to the Gestapo
   d. That Captain Trehn will discover that he's been dipping into the hotel's till

III. True or False

1. Leopold Schmendrick designed the Nilpferd.
2. Olivia Quaile used to be Ingrid's governess.
3. Frau Freya Frage knows that Hama Tartus slept with Gelda Pourboire.
4. Captain Trehn is about to arrest the Diederichs.
5. Wayne Radford and Basil Naunton are responsible for Kurt Krauss's financial troubles.
6. Captain Trehn was never a passenger on the Nilpferd.
7. Marty Hollands disguised himself as a mailman when he first visited the Diederichs.
8. Olivia Quaile shared a table with Joslyn Frank at dinner last night.
9. Gelda Pourboire lost her job in Kiel because of Kurt Krauss.
10. Felix Frage drank brandy.

IV. Reading Between the Lines

1. Which of the following are *not* red herrings? (You may check as many as you wish.)
   a. Schleswig-Holstein
   b. z-100
   c. The submarine base
   d. The midget
   e. The Everglade Land Company
   f. The Hotel Splendide
   g. The tray
   h. The nightclub
   i. The Nilpferd
   j. The R, S, and T boats
   k. The radio
   l. The beer
   m. The map
   n. The cookbook

2. Who killed Kurt Krauss?

3. What was the motive for killing Kurt Krauss?

4. When did the killer decide to kill him?

5. How did the killer kill him?

6. What reason did each of the five suspects have for confessing to the murder?
   a. Professor Diederich
   b. Ingrid Diederich
   c. Marty Hollands
   d. Olivia Quaile
   e. Leopold Schmendrick

The answers to the quiz are in the back of the book. Before you figure out your score, read on to learn what really happened to Kurt Krauss, and why.

The Truth

Here we have a situation, rare in fiction, not so rare in life, in which the villain and the victim are the same person. Kurt Krauss was murdered but, before he was murdered, Kurt Krauss earned it.

Which of his many villainies led to the violent departure of this feared and hated man? Let us go back nearly six years, to the beginning of the Nazi era in Germany and the rise of Kurt Krauss as a supremely important critic, producer and political figure, living in Hamburg, enjoying his importance. Among those receiving the favor of Krauss's patronage and friendship was a corrupt police officer named Wilhelm Trehn, whom Krauss treated with amusement, as a kind of tame ape. Krauss liked to invite Trehn to parties and introduce him to important people almost as a pet, his house gangster. Trehn played along for the contacts it afforded him among the powerful people of society.

Not long after the Nazis took power, a friend of Krauss's wanted a post at the University of Kiel, which was then held by Professor Rudolf Diederich, a naval scientist at work on advanced underwater craft. Krauss denounced Diederich anonymously to his friends in the Nazi hierarchy, and Diederich, a widower, lost his post and was placed under house arrest with his daughter Ingrid.

About a year later, Krauss bought movie rights to three novels, thrillers, written by a young American, Marty Hollands. The negotiation was transatlantic, Hollands at that time having never been to Europe.

Shortly after this business dealing with Marty Hollands, Krauss met Gelda Pourboire, a French singer/actress with a checkered past. She had, in fact, had an earlier affair with Professor Diederich three years before, when she had thought briefly of settling down. She was living with police officer Wilhelm Trehn when she met Krauss, but immediately switched to Krauss, as being much more useful to her in her career. Trehn, bored with Gelda by then, hadn't minded a bit.

Around the time he took up with Gelda Pourboire, Kurt Krauss also first had dealings with Leopold Schmendrick, a naval architect. Schmendrick had a good reputation as a designer of pleasure boats, and had known naval scientist Professor Rudolf Diederich socially before the period of Diederich's house arrest. Krauss hired Schmendrick to design a new yacht for him, to be called the Nilpferd.

Also around the same time, Krauss met the British journalist Joslyn Frank, who had come to Kiel partly to interview Krauss for a London magazine and partly to do research on the Schleswig-Holstein Question for a book she was planning. The Schleswig-Holstein Question was also the hobby of Professor Diederich, he having published some small pieces on the affair, and Joslyn Frank wanted to meet him, but found it impossible, because of the Professor's house arrest. But then Kurt Krauss unexpectedly used his influence and made the meeting possible, and Joslyn Frank and Professor Diederich had a pleasant afternoon discussing this most vexing Question in the history of European royalty.

Schleswig and Holstein were two duchys linked as one. This "indissoluble" link had been affirmed in 1640 by the Danish king Christian I in the charter of Ribe. Their relationship had been with the Danish crown, but Holstein also later developed relationships with the German confederation of states. With the extinction of the male line of the reigning house of Denmark by the death of King Frederick VII on November 15, 1863, the famous Question arose. The royal succession in Denmark could pass through females, but Schleswig and Holstein were still under Salic law, which forbids females to carry the royal line, which would mean the succession in those two duchys would pass to the dukes of Augustenburg. The Question of the succession opened the whole question of relationships, Schleswig preferring its link to Denmark and Holstein preferring its link to Germany. England and other European powers entered to muddy the waters and keep either side from gaining too much power, which led to an impasse, which eventually Bismarck used as an opportunity for a war with Denmark which ended with Schleswig and Holstein both being added to Germany.

Joslyn Frank's view of this Question was expressed in the title of her book: *Who Cares Who Killed Schleswig-Holstein?*, in which she presented the argument that disputes of historical right and wrong are irrelevant, reality supersedes morality. Professor Diederich, who takes the Question much more seriously, was saddened by the book when it came out.

On the other hand, Kurt Krauss was furious when the interview with him appeared. Joslyn Frank had not let his favor in setting up the meeting with Diederich affect her journalistic independence, and it was a rough article indeed.

The following year, 1936, was the time of the famous Berlin Olympics. Kurt Krauss attended, of
course, and met there Wayne Radford and Basil
Naunton, a pair of conmen pretending to be simple
sportsmen. They explain to potential suckers that
they no longer have to work since they invested in
the Everglade Land Company in Florida, in the U.S.
Krauss fell for their elaborate scam and put every
pfennig he could find into it, which meant he had to
default on his debt to Marty Hollands for those three
books he'd bought and made movies out of; but he
expected to pay Hollands later, when the Everglade
Land Company money started pouring in, and in the
meantime, what could Hollands do, far away in
America?

Gelda Pourboire was with Krauss at the Olympics,
of course, and her naturally roving eye was combined
with irritation at Krauss for having done nothing at
all to help her career. Partly for fun, and partly for
spite, she had it off with both Radford and Naunton,
separately, during the Olympics.

After the Olympics, Krauss invited his new
friends, Radford and Naunton, to join him for a cruise
on the recently completed Nilpferd. Gelda came along
as well. Her relationship with the Nilpferd was already extensive. She'd seen it in drydock before it
was finished, had met Leopold Schmendrick and
liked his shy little-boy qualities, and had seduced
him in a completed cabin aboard the incompleted
ship.

This was the Nilpferd's third sailing. On the first,
already irritated at Krauss's refusal to be useful,
Gelda went out of her way to have a quick fling with
one of the seamen on the crew, one Hama Tartus, a

stateless person who had worked on tramp steamers around the world for years before jumping ship a few years before in Kiel. And on the Nilpferd's second sailing, Gelda's target of opportunity became a friend of Hama Tartus's on the crew, the cook, Felix Frage.

On the third cruise, containing Gelda and the two conmen, tragedy struck. One night, Hama Tartus was awakened by the sound of scuffling, and went to the galley to find Felix Frage dead, Krauss standing over him with a frying pan. Krauss explained he'd just learned Felix was an American spy. Harboring a spy could make terrible trouble for Krauss, he said, so he'd decided to offer to run Felix across the North Sea to the coast of Scotland and leave him there. But when he confronted Frage, the man attacked him. Krauss asked Hama Tartus's help in concealing the death, and Tartus was too scared and confused to refuse.

Back in Hamburg, Hama Tartus told the false story to Felix Frage's widow, Frau Freya Frage, who was the housekeeper for Professor Diederich and his daughter and was one of the very few people admitted into the Diederich's house. Frau Freya Frage knew at once the story was a lie, though she didn't believe Hama Tartus was lying to her, but was repeating a falsehood he believed to be true.

Frau Freya Frage had two reasons for knowing the story of Felix's death was false. In the first place, Felix drank very little, and *never* drank brandy, because it gave him heartburn. And in the second place, she knew that Felix was a low-level spy for American Intelligence, and so she took it for granted that his spying activities had caught up with him and that he'd been murdered. She never told anyone her suspicions, including Hama.

Shortly after Hama Tartus testified at the official inquisition into the disappearance of Felix Frage, corroborating Krauss's story, Hama went to Krauss and told him the incident had made him very nervous and he didn't ever want to go to sea again. Hama had some money saved and wanted to buy a hotel. Krauss agreed to help finance him, just so the hotel was outside Germany. Hama knew this was almost a bribe and almost blackmail, and felt guilty and nervous about it, but he wanted the chance to make something of himself. The Hotel Kuckkuckuhr was then for sale, and Hama bought it, with Krauss as his silent partner. Frau Freya Frage came along to manage the hotel, and she and Hama Tartus are now very close, but cannot marry, because without Felix Frage's body he cannot be declared dead.

Around this time, Krauss's checks from the Everglade Land Company stopped, with a brief final note saying the company was being reorganized. Krauss had stretched himself to the limit to buy into that scheme and, as he then told Hama Tartus, he was suddenly so broke he wished he had back the money he'd given Hama. But that had gone for the hotel, so all he could hope was that the hotel would soon make a profit.

It was then, with his finances in a shambles and the slowly growing realization that he was a victim of a con—he never was sure whether Radford and Naunton were conmen or fellow victims—that Krauss discovered that his girl friend, Gelda Pourboire, had been forging his name to checks, having decided that if he wasn't going to help her one way, he could help her another. If Krauss hadn't suddenly gone broke, he would never have known about it. As it was, he was so angry he preferred charges, Gelda was quickly prosecuted and found guilty, and actually served six months before a friendly lawyer got her off. Krauss had blackballed her in Germany, so she returned to France to work.

At the same time, there were debts Krauss couldn't pay, though he would never admit the truth to anybody, but would merely stonewall. One of these was Leopold Schmendrick's bill for the design and construction of the Nilpferd; Krauss stalled him for almost two years, until Schmendrick finally sued, a few months ago. But as soon as he started court action against Krauss, the Gestapo took an interest in Schmendrick because of his old political activity under Weimar. Clearly Krauss was behind this persecution. Schmendrick was forced to flee the country, arriving here at the Kuckkuckuhr about three months ago. He and Hama Tartus had known one another slightly years ago in Kiel, and Hama remembered how decent Schmendrick had been at that time to a simple sailor, so Schmendrick was invited to stay on even after his money ran out.

Meantime, Marty Hollands had come to Germany for the first time. As it happened, Hollands was then also becoming interested in the Schleswig-Holstein Question as the setting for a mystery novel to be called *Stain on the Pedigree,* so he combined research with a quest for justice and visited Germany, to sue Krauss for his money, only to learn that Krauss was too powerful to be successfully sued in a German court.

On the train across France and into Germany, Marty Hollands met Gelda Pourboire, returning to a job in Kiel for the first time since her trouble with

Kurt Krauss. Gelda and Marty liked one another and had a pleasant two days and two nights on the train.

Marty Hollands' frustration with German law versus Kurt Krauss was echoed in frustration in his research about the Schleswig-Holstein Question. He too wanted to interview Professor Diederich, but was stopped. However, Marty was naturally an adventurer, devil-may-care. Disguising himself as the mailman, he got into the Diederich house and met both the Professor and Ingrid. He was quite taken with Ingrid, but she was too depressed because of their circumstances to notice him.

Marty returned several times to the Professor's house, disguised as the water meter-reader, the butcher's delivery boy, the plumber to fix a broken toilet, and so on. Finally, he convinced them to let him rescue them both, and they made their surreptitious way out of Germany and here to the Kuckkuckuhr, where Frau Freya Frage, the Diederich's former housekeeper, had said she would make them welcome.

Only one person present at the Kuckkuckuhr has not had previous dealings with Kurt Krauss, and that's Miss Olivia Quaile. She, however, has known several of the other players in our drama. A retired nanny whose hobby is collecting recipes for a fish cookbook, she came to Europe several years ago and soon made the acquaintance of Felix Frage, a seacook who could be of obvious help to her in her researches. Felix introduced her to his wife, Frau Freya Frage, who, though she knew her husband was a spy, never suspected that beneath her sweet-little-old-lady exterior, Olivia Quaile was also a spy, and that the fish cookbook was a cover for Miss Quaile's search for a suspected new Nazi submarine factory. Felix also introduced Miss Quaile, with her cover story, to his friend Hama Tartus.

More recently, Miss Quaile met Joslyn Frank at lunch in a *Gasthaus* in the little coastal German town of Schönberg. Joslyn was there as a journalist, this time trying to do a piece for the *American Mercury* on the secret buildup of Nazi military force. Joslyn attached herself to the little old lady, considering Miss Quaile good cover for her own journalistic snooping, unaware that the shoe was really on the other foot.

During this last period of time in Germany, Miss Quaile had been staying at the Hotel Splendide in Kiel—Joslyn was in a different hotel in the same city—and met Marty Hollands there, during the time Marty was visiting the Diederichs in disguise. The two conmen/sportsmen, Wayne Radford and Basil Naunton, were staying in the same hotel at the same time, and chatted up Miss Quaile out of habit; both the fake sportsmen and the fake nanny are professionally gregarious.

Having discovered at last the location of the secret submarine factory, Miss Quaile came to this hotel in Switzerland because she was to meet her contact here, pass on the information, and leave it to the contact to get the information back to the United States and her brother, the spymaster Quentin Quaile. Joslyn Frank accompanied her because Kurt Krauss had arranged to have Joslyn's visa revoked; it didn't matter where she went, just so it was out of Germany within 24 hours.

Gelda Pourboire had also been driven from Germany by Kurt Krauss, and was on her way to a possible singing job in Geneva when the storm stranded her here. The conmen, Radford and Naunton, were

also just passing through. As for Captain Wilhelm
Trehn, he had come to the hotel because here in
Switzerland he's once again up to his old tricks,
though on a more modest scale. Many refugees move
through Switzerland these days, many of them with
dubious or non-existent papers, and Trehn preys
upon them, demanding bribes or he will arrange for
arrests and deportations. Occasionally, some help-
less person can't afford to buy off Captain Trehn,
and those people do get sent back to places where
they don't want to be. That unhappy fate is about to
happen to Leopold Schmendrick, even though Hama
Tartus begged Captain Trehn to show poor Schmendrick mercy.

In fact, Hama Tartus himself is another victim of
Trehn's extortion. A stateless person from the Lev-
ant, Hama Tartus has never had proper papers, and
has been paying off Captain Trehn almost since they
both arrived here in Switzerland, getting the money
by embezzling from the hotel, unknown to his partner, Kurt Krauss. When Krauss arrived at the
Kuckkuckuhr just ahead of the storm, Hama and
Freya assumed he'd found out about the embezzle-
ments and was here to cause trouble.

Who killed Kurt Krauss? Five people have confessed, and they can't all be right. Are they all wrong?

Let's begin with those who did *not* confess. Freya
Frage and Hama Tartus have reason to fear Krauss,
should he find out that they've been stealing from
the hotel to pay off Captain Trehn, but that hasn't
actually happened, and if it does Hama still has his
knowledge of the circumstances of the death of Felix
Frage to help protect him against Krauss, and in any
event these are both rather timid people, unlikely to

take such an extreme action unless really and truly driven to it. Nor would they murder someone by poisoning him in their own hotel with their own food. So their motive isn't good enough, and their opportunity is too good.

Joslyn Frank has only professional trouble with Krauss. He's an irritation, a thorn in her side, but a crusading journalist learns to live with such things. As for Gelda, her emotional life is such that, if she were going to murder men who had wronged her, she'd have emptied Europe by now. Gelda thinks of today, not of yesterday.

Wayne Radford and Basil Naunton might have a little trouble with Kurt Krauss if he ever learned they were conmen who'd fleeced him, but he's given them no clear indication that he knows the truth, and in any event their style is to slip and slide and disappear, not to attack.

Captain Trehn, secure in his power in this remote corner of Switzerland, has no motive at all. Even if Krauss learns that Hama Tartus has been embezzling from the hotel to pay off Trehn, what could he do to Trehn? Nothing.

Which leaves the five who confessed: Marty Hollands, Professor Rudolf Diederich, Ingrid Diederich, Leopold Schmendrick and Miss Olivia Quaile. Which of them is telling the truth?

In a way, none of them.

Marty Hollands' gallant gesture is easily seen through. Afraid that Ingrid had slipped the poison into Krauss's food during a sham faint, he immediately confessed the crime himself to protect her. The same motive is true of the Professor's confession; both men thought Ingrid the murderess.

Were they right? No. Ingrid was also being gallant, thinking it was her father who had poisoned Krauss, and confessing in order to protect him from the law. All three quickly sorted out the confusions and retracted their confessions, and were given a stern talking-to by Captain Trehn.

Leopold Schmendrick had just been arrested by Captain Trehn. He faced deportation and probable death in Germany. His current problems were much more severe than any past injustices committed against him by Kurt Krauss. When the word came that Krauss had been murdered, however, he immediately realized that if he confessed to the crime he wouldn't be deported, wouldn't die in a Nazi concentration camp, but would be kept in Switzerland, would be tried for murder, with luck would be found guilty, and would spend the next several years in a relatively comfortable Swiss jail. This seemed to him his only hope for survival, and so he maintained his guilt throughout the episode.

Which leaves Miss Olivia Quaile, who had never met Kurt Krauss before, and who barely gives any sensible reason for having murdered him, and yet ...

She done it.

Miss Quaile's contact, to whom she was supposed to pass on the information about the location of the secret submarine factory, was the midget with Rundelman's Circus. When, just before dinner, she learned from the sportsmen that the midget had been arrested by the German police, just shy of the Swiss border, she knew her own cover must be blown as well—or would be almost immediately, when the Gestapo used their famous methods in questioning the midget—and that only the storm had kept the

German Secret Police from pursuing her here already. She knew she had to accomplish two things, and both at once: She must put herself somewhere that German agents couldn't get at her. And she must pass on to her brother somehow the name of the location of the submarine factory.

It was during dinner, talking with Leopold, as he described to her what he knew of the villainies of Kurt Krauss, that Miss Quaile got her idea. She herself had long suspected that Krauss had had something to do with the mysterious disappearance of her fellow spy, Felix Frage. Going to Krauss's table, showing him her map, she slipped the poison into his food exactly as she said in her confession, but for reasons she didn't admit.

Arrested by the Swiss police, she would be safe from German assassination teams. And when Quentin received her message, asking him to contact her lawyer, Ulysses Schönberg, he would know there was no such lawyer and that the name had to be a message. She'd been looking for the coastal town where submarines were being made. There is a coastal town called Schönberg, where she first met Joslyn Frank. She would be safe, and her message would get through.

Eventually the storm surrounding the Kuckkuckuhr abated, the road up the mountain was cleared, and Swiss federal police arrived. By that time, Marty Hollands and the Diederichs had sorted out their misunderstandings and had all retracted their confessions. When, immediately after the federal police, a group of strong young Americans, vacationing skiers, also arrived at the hotel, with greetings for Miss Olivia Quaile from her brother Quentin, she announced she must have had a funny spell, and retracted *her* confession.

Next, Hama Tartus begged Marty to help Leopold
Schmendrick, explaining the man's background, and
Marty promised to hire the best attorney in Zürich
to fight Schmendrick's deportation. Professor
Diederich also swore to vouch for Schmendrick's
probity and to recommend him as a fine naval architect to any potential employer. When Schmendrick heard all this, he too recanted his confession,
and so, from five confessions, the police were left
with none.

They did, however, have certain evidence. Hama
Tartus and Frau Freya Frage told the police that
Captain Wilhelm Trehn had come into the kitchen
during dinner, demanding to know which plates con-
tained Kurt Krauss's food, and was left briefly alone
with them. Marty Hollands, who had been Trehn's
tablemate at dinner, confirmed that Trehn had gone
to the kitchen for a while and had come back looking
very satisfied with himself. The Diederichs and Joslyn Frank and Gelda Pourboire all described the obviously hostile confrontation between Kurt Krauss
and Captain Trehn when Trehn had arrived for dinner. And the Swiss police were reminded of the cor-
ruption charges against Trehn back in Kiel, where
Trehn had been a frequent companion of Kurt
Krauss.

Looking at the evidence against himself, realizing
just how few friends he had made among the people
around him, Captain Trehn calculated his odds and
escaped into the night, down the mountainside,
swearing vengeance. He was never heard from again.

As to the others, Hama and Freya remained happily at the Kuckkuckuhr together the rest of their
lives, and Joslyn Frank made her reputation as a

war correspondent in the Pacific a few years later. Her autobiography, *Dateline: Anywhere,* was a major seller both in America and Great Britain.

All the others made their way to the United States before war broke out. Wayne Radford and Basil Naunton met a fellow on the ship going home who was just starting a professional football team, and they became his partners and prospered mightily. They were true sportsmen now, but they never entirely gave up being conmen: For the rest of their lives, they would move their franchised team to a new city every three years, receiving generous under-the-table payments from their new hosts each time. At last, they and their team settled in Florida, not far from the Everglade Land Company that had started it all.

Leopold Schmendrick finished out his days designing yachts in Santa Barbara, California. Marty Hollands' historical novel, *Stain on the Pedigree,* did so miserably that he never wrote another historical, and therefore lived happily ever after with his wife, Ingrid.

Herr Professor Rudolf Diederich was hired by Yale University upon his arrival in America. However, absent-mindedly, he showed up at Harvard instead. No one noticed the mistake, and he spent the rest of his life there, nodding at Harvard Yard and saying, "So this is Yale."

When the story of the murder of Kurt Krauss was made into a movie by Warner Brothers in 1940, called "Hugh Fong At Murder Hotel," Gelda Pourboire played herself, which led to minor Hollywood stardom, in which she played spies and femmes fatales for several years, until she married an Oklahoma oilman and settled into contented retirement.

And Miss Olivia Quaile astounded everybody including herself by finishing her fish cookbook which, with the title *Underwater Gourmet,* went on to be a major bestseller, on the proceeds of which she really did retire.

Or so she said.

I. Matching

1–j; 2–i; 3–a; 4–d; 5–k; 6–g; 7–c; 8–b; 9–e; 10–h
11–f

Give yourself two points for each correct answer.

Maximum score: 22

II. Multiple Choice

1–c; 2–d; 3–b; 4–b; 5–a; 6–d; 7–c; 8–b; 9–d; 10–a

GIve yourself five points for each correct answer.

Maximum score: 50

III. True or False

1–T; 2–F; 3–F; 4–F; 5–T; 6–T; 7–T; 8–F; 9–T;
10–F

Give yourself three points for each correct
answer. Maximum score: 30

IV. 1. The four non-red herrings are: c, d, m, n.
Give yourself five points for each correct guess.
Subtract five points for each incorrect guess.
2. Olivia Quaile. If you guessed correctly, take
25 points
3. Because her contact (the midget) had been
arrested, and only by getting herself arrested
could she hope to get the name of the town containing the submarine base (Schönberg) to her
spymaster brother, Quentin Quaile. (10 points)

Answers to the Quiz

4. She decided on a dramatic and newsworthy murder before dinner, when she learned about the arrest of the midget. During dinner she picked her victim—the greatest Nazi present. (10 points)

5. She killed him with the poison she carried in a bottle of lavendar scented cologne, just as she described it in her confession. (10 points)

6. a. The professor confessed to protect Ingrid, whom he suspected of having done the deed.
(5 points)

b. Ingrid confessed to protect her father, whom she suspected of having done the deed.
(5 points)

c. Marty confessed to protect Ingrid, whom he suspected of having done the deed. (5 points)

d. Leopold confessed because he knew he'd be safer in a Swiss prison, held for murder, than being shipped back to Germany. (5 points)

e. Olivia confessed so she could send the vital information to her brother under the guise of asking for her lawyer, and so that she would be in custody and safe from pursuing German agents. (Quentin would know she had no lawyer named Schönberg. And in a telegram the "lawyer's" first name, Ulysses, would be abbreviated to its initial; U, as in U-boat.)
(5 points)

Maximum score: 100

The highest possible score is 202.

Anything over 150: Sherlock Holmes
Over 100: Detective First Grade
Over 65: Detective Second Grade
Over 45: Detective Third Grade
Under 45: Inspector Clouzot

The first three sections, for a maximum of 102 points, test your attentiveness and powers of observation. If you scored well—over 70—on this part of the quiz, you may congratulate yourself on being a good witness. (No one's going to put anything over on you!) The final section, *Reading Between the Lines,* measures your deductive skills. If you did better than 50 out of 100 here, you can take pride in being an exceptionally astute problem solver—and possibly a bit of a psychic as well.